CYN NO MORE

Thirsting for Blood Series ~ Book Three

a novel by

Sue Dent

This edition of Cyn No More is published by

S D Enterprises
ISBN 978-0-9960121-2-6

Acknowledgments

Thanks to all who enjoy my little tales
as I write them for you.
Thanks also to my second publisher for
helping out with the edits.
You know who you are, Frank Creed!
Thanks also to my "hippie" friend, and
fantastic editor, Deborah Cullins Smith.
Also, thanks to my UK Cabbie friends
(from facebook)
Bill Tompkins and Peter Martin
for providing actual excerpts for my books.
I like to be accurate when I can.
I hope y'all enjoy this little addition to my
Thirsting for Blood Series as much
as I enjoyed writing it!

Watch for the Black Bed Sheet Books editions coming out soon!

CYN NO MORE

By
Sue Dent

S D Enterprises * Ridgeland MS

Other Books by Sue Dent:

Never Ceese

Forever Richard

Electric Angel

Coming Soon

Penny for Your Thoughts

Voodoo Cowboy

For naturally blood will be of kind. Drawn-
to blood, where he may it find.

English priest John Lydgate

Prologue

THE HORSE-DRAWN CART CREAKED loudly as sixteen-year-old Brendan climbed into the wagon box. It shifted to one side when he sat. "She shouldn't be left alone," he scowled.

Raewyn stood from her seat across from Brendan, separated her brawling younger brothers Christian and Rolland, praised eight-year-old Sophie for sitting quietly, and then turned her attention to Brendan. "Keep your voice down. Mother and Father will hear. They're not that far away."

Richard, older than Brendan by two years, turned in the buckboard seat at the front of the wagon. "Father wouldn't leave Mother alone if he thought she wouldn't be safe. Besides, going to services this afternoon and leaving Mother to tend to her roses without any distractions is our birthday gift to her. Or did that slip your mind? We all agreed."

"I'm just telling you how I feel."

"But we all talked about this *before* we made the decision. If you took issue with the matter or even had a better idea, you should've spoken up sooner."

"No one would have listened to me," he groused. "No one ever listens to me."

Richard shushed him. "Here comes Father now. Don't spoil things for everyone else."

Father grinned favorably at those in the cart as he stepped up and took the reins from Richard. "She's going to love her time alone. What a perfect gift the six of you have given her." Placing his tongue against his teeth, Father clucked the mare into motion.

* * *

Julia held back tears as her family pulled away but forced herself to regroup after she no longer heard the creaking of the wagon wheels; the steady plod of their mare pulling it. They would be back soon enough, and until then, she would enjoy this free time. After all, Merideth and the children had planned this time alone for her. She would not spoil it by being sad.

* * *

Two days later, the family loaded down a larger cart provided by the mission with all their belongings.

"I'm sorry," one parishioner said to Merideth. "If we could find the wolf that attacked your wife—"

Merideth placed an understanding hand on the man's shoulder. "It wouldn't make any difference. I was considering the opportunity in Port Hampton anyway. It's by the sea, and I miss it so." His brief smile faded as quickly as it came.

Cyn No More

"But to have you leave under these circumstances," the parishioner said with a look of regret.

Meri shook his head back and forth. "No one could have anticipated this. It isn't your fault."

Richard overheard the exchange of words and turned to Brendan. "See, no one could have known what was going to happen."

"I knew," Brendan said, tormented by what he had not told anyone. "And I should have done something."

* * *

They arrived at Port Hampton within a week and attended a gathering put together by parishioners to welcome the family. An anxious Brendan found Richard in the main hall and insisted that he follow him outside.

Presently, that's all Richard could remember as he sat up, his clothes soaked through to his skin. Had he fallen in the river that rushed along behind him? He pushed down with his palms to try and stand but cried out when blistered flesh came into contact with the ground.

He turned toward the sound of someone pushing through the brush. Brendan arrived and knelt next to him. "I brought something for your hands," he said, taking charge. He applied salve, and then settled back on his heels.

Richard studied Brendan's expression. "What

happened to me?"

"You fell into the river."

He made it sound so trivial. Too trivial.

"One doesn't just fall into the river." A rope lay on the ground nearby, a knot tied at one end. Richard's eyes grew wide at a troubling memory.

"I was pulled in." He glanced at the Mill Creek Bridge. "You sent me up there to wait for Dalia to float down—" He jerked his head back to face Brendan. "Is she all right? Is little Dalia safe?"

"She's fine. I sent her back to the mission with her sister Isabelle."

Richard looked at the rope again. Brendan had been in such a despondent mood over the past few days. "Why the hangman's noose? When you gave me the rope—it had one tied in it. I remember now that I wanted to ask you about that."

"I wasn't trying to kill myself if that's what you think. And it's only called a hangman's noose if you intend to hang someone with it. I wasn't planning on hanging anyone."

"Then what?"

"I know something. Something you wouldn't believe. I was setting a trap with the rope."

"What were you hoping to trap?"

"Not what. Who. The one who hurt mother. The one

who scratched her."

"You're mad! A wolf attacked Mother. Anything else is a lie."

"It isn't a lie. Joachim told me—"

"Who is Joachim'?"

"A . . . friend. Why?"

"Because, Brother, the truth is only as good as the one telling it. If I don't know of whom you speak, then why should I put stock in his words? How do you know this-this Joachim isn't lying? Father said we shouldn't speak of Mother's attack, and so we shouldn't. I promise," he added, "I will not hesitate to tell Father how I nearly drowned at your hands if you don't keep quiet about what you say you know."

Brendan didn't answer. His eyes darted from the ground to the sky to a nearby tree. Richard had never known his brother to consider anything for so long.

"All right," Brendan sneered. "I promise."

"And you'll never speak of the matter again?"

"Yes," he hissed.

"Good. Then we should be getting back to the mission."

Sue Dent

Port Hampton, Wales, 1790 Five Years Later

Richard rushed out of the house after Father. "Please don't leave me alone with her."

Father turned on a heel. "There's no point trying to get me to change my mind. My decision is final. I'm taking everyone to the service tonight and leaving you here to look after your sister."

The setting sun dipped closer toward the horizon creating cold pockets of long shadows. Standing in one of those pockets, Richard drew his coatless arms tight to his body. "You have to know this will end badly." *Most likely for me.*

"The two of you need to work through your differences."

He's gone mad! "You know she doesn't listen to me."

"We'll be back after services." Father turned to head toward the horse-drawn cart.

"Don't," Richard pleaded, "leave me with that—that—*her*. It certainly makes more sense to take me along. What will you be teaching on tonight? Perhaps I can help. Let Raewyn stay behind instead. At least the urchin lis—" Father turned, tightlipped, and eyes a-glare. Richard quickly reworded. "I mean—child . . . at least the—umm—*child* listens to Raewyn."

Cyn No More

It wasn't easy to forget six-year-old Ceese pouring ink all over his notes just the other day, claiming the action to be an accident even though Richard saw her deliberately swat at the bottle and then smile afterward.

Meri's tight lips curled upwards. "Perhaps then," he said, "you can draw some ideas on how to handle Cee Cee from Raewyn's success."

All at once, Ceese rushed out of the house, across the front porch and down the two steps. She grabbed hold of Father's right leg and held tight. "I want to go with you. Please don't leave me with him."

"There. You see," Richard said with some relief, "the feeling is mutual. And you know you don't want to disappoint her." Father coddled her more than he ever did any of the other children. Being the oldest, Richard bore witness to this, and he was quick to play to Father's weakness.

Meri reached down, lifted the girl up, and in a stern yet gentle voice said, "Richard is going to stay with you tonight, and I don't want to hear another word about it. It would make me very sad if I knew you were upset about this arrangement. You don't want me to leave sad, do you?"

"I don't want you to leave at all," she pouted. "Not without me."

Mother stepped down from the cart and moved next to Father. "You'll be good for *Risiart*, won't you? No trouble?" Though it had been six years, Mother still struggled with the trauma of the attack by the wolf. Ceese, born nine months later, distressed her even more. At times, she distanced herself from Ceese because of the attached memories, but it was getting more comfortable for her, Richard could tell.

Ceese pushed her bottom lip out.

"I need you to do this for me," Father encouraged.

The girl sighed pitifully. "Only because you ask."

"That's my Cee Cee. Now run along back inside before you catch your death." At the sound of the front door shutting, Father said to Richard. "We shan't be gone long—an hour or two at best."

"A lifetime," Richard let slip, thinking his parents too far away to hear. But Father turned in response. "A *lively* time," Richard reworded. "—I'm sure we'll have a good and *lively* time."

The wagon creaked out of sight. Richard headed inside to find that Ceese had put herself to bed. *Perhaps the urchin will pass the evening by ignoring me.* Richard smiled at his possible good fortune.

With an hour safely tucked away, it became clear to him that Ceese might do just as he hoped; that she would hide away until Father, and the others returned. But seconds later, her terrified scream launched him from his seat and took him away from his studies. He raced across the room, and threw the bedroom door open. Ceese cowered in the furthest corner.

"Bad dream?"

She pointed, whispered. "S—someone is at the window. It's him. He's come for me."

What the devil is she talking about? "Who has come for you?"

Richard moved to the window but saw no one. He heard odd, scratching noises and even growling. Something was trying to get in. He turned his head toward the back door and then motioned for her to come to him. "I'll lower you down." He unlocked and slid the bedroom window open. "Go hide. And stay hidden until I come after you. Do you understand?"

"What if he kills you?"

He drew back at the comment. *Is she actually worried about this?* "I'm fairly certain I'll be fine."

She hugged his neck tightly as he lowered her down. On the ground and staring up, she said, "I'll climb up one of the bigger ash trees. He can't touch me there. He can't go near them."

Play along, he thought. There certainly didn't seem to be time for anything else. What an odd thing for her to say, though. "Yes, fine—the ash tree then. Run along."

* * *

Perched on a lower limb, Ceese huddled close to the

trunk, curled up and shivering. The sound of her family returning, the hooves of the mare plodding along, and the creak of the wagon, brought her to life and she scampered down.

"Meri," Julia gasped and pointed from where she sat next to her husband.

Meri saw what looked like his youngest running toward the wagon. "Cee Cee!" He pulled the reins tight, called for his second oldest to take them from him. "You children stay here. Brendan's in charge." Brendan moved to the buckboard seat next to Mother. Raewyn, Sophie, Christian, and Rolland sat obediently in the back.

Meri jumped down just in time to accommodate Ceese's lunge into his arms. He made shushing noises to calm her and drew her into his shoulder. "What are you doing out? You should be in bed. Where's Richard?"

Julia arrived at Meri's side and draped her shawl over Ceese's shoulders.

"I d—don't know," Ceese stuttered, her teeth chattering so that she barely got the words out. "Richard t-told me to hide until it was s—safe.

"Why would he tell you to do that?"

"To protect me."

"From what? Certainly not from the cold. We'll be lucky if you haven't caught your death already."

Cyn No More

"There was a man at my window. And then he came into the house."

They all turned to see Richard stagger out onto the porch, one hand on the back of his head, the other clutching the porches side rail. Ceese squirmed down and ran toward him. She reached him just as he sank to the first step.

"You're alive," and she wrapped grateful arms around his neck."

"What happened?" Father asked, coming to stand in front of the two. "Are you all right?"

"There was an intruder, but it seems he's gone now. I searched the house."

"But the house isn't that large, Richard, and it's clear Ceese has been outside for more than just the time it took to search it."

"Yes. Of course, I must've been knocked out."

"This intruder? Did you get a look at him?"

"He attacked me as I left the girls' room, so I hardly had the chance. I do remember his eyes, though. They had a hard green-gold cast to them like nothing I've ever seen before, at least not on a human. They were like an animal's eyes—a dog or wolf or something like that." Julia gasped. "He's gone now," Richard said, addressing her fear, "and probably just someone looking for food."

11

"Is that blood?" Father asked of the hand Richard touched to his head.

Richard stared numbly. "Yes, I suppose it is. Fancy that."

"Did he scratch you?"

Confused brows knitted. Had Father just asked him that? "No, just hit me." He felt the back of his head again and winced, "And with something very hard from the size of the knot."

Meri nodded away the awkwardness of his question. "Yes, of course." He then reached to take Ceese. "Come with me," he said, holding his arms out, "so Mother can tend to Richard's wound."

"No," Ceese said, clasped Richard's neck tighter. "I want to stay with him. He needs me."

Raewyn took charge. "How about you be his nurse. You can help me gather the things we need to dress Richard's wound."

Her eyes rounded. "Yes, I'd like that."

Meri commented after the front door closed behind the pair, "At least the two of you are getting along now."

"If only I'd known it would take me nearly being killed to get her to warm up to me."

"The notion of self-sacrifice," Father said, "can be a compelling persuader. But I don't think I have to

Cyn No More

remind you of that."

* * *

A month later, Richard sat at his desk and rubbed at tired eyes. The flickering glow of a nearby lantern kept darker shadows at bay. He considered the organized mess in front of him as he prepared for his ordination the following day, but the clutter distracted. He pulled notes together, sorted, and stacked them. Lastly, he took up Father's Gaelic Bible to return it to its box, but something caught his eye. With careful fingers, he prised open and folded back two flaps of wood. *A false bottom?* Inside and folded neatly, a set of preaching bands—torn and stained with dried blood? He took them out for a closer look. *Why the devil did he keep these? And why here?*

A sudden rush of wind on an otherwise calm night took his attention. He peered out the window in front of him to see leaves scattering in the wake of a random gust.

He stared so intently that a knock at the door startled him into dropping the bands altogether. He jumped to stand, tipped his desk, then rushed to steady it before it toppled over.

Brendan stopped stoking the fire to guffaw at his brother's flailing his limbs. "Should I answer that, or do you have your wits about you now?"

Richard shook off his initial shock and stood. "I've got it."

13

Sue Dent

He spent a few moments with the stranger before turning to Brendan. "This gentleman needs someone to read last rites to a dying friend, and since Father isn't here, I'm going to do it." Father, Mother, and sisters Raewyn and Sophie had gone off to assist a parishioner in need of a midwife.

The door to the girls' room creaked open, and a sleepy-eyed Ceese peeked out. "Evil," she hissed under her breath. "He's evil."

Richard took his coat from a hook and slid into it. "You do whatever Brendan says," he told Ceese.

"You're not going anywhere," Brendan fired back at Richard. "Father left you in charge. He'll blame me if something goes wrong in your absence."

"What could go wrong? Just put Ceese back to bed. I won't be gone long. I'm sure you can handle things until I return."

Richard pulled the door closed in the face of Brendan's protest.

* * *

On his back, Richard stared up and blinked heavy eyelids to clear his vision, squinted and frowned at the twisted, gnarled network of branches above. The forest canopy proved so thick; he couldn't see the night sky beyond. *Where am I, and why am I here?* With some effort, he recalled having words with Brendan. But the disagreement he recalled was much earlier in the day

14

or perhaps some other day. His foggy state of mind left him uncertain.

He inhaled deeply and then coughed at the suffocating odors of dank earth and decaying leaves. The repugnant stench of death from some unseen and no doubt maggot-infested carcass made him reconsider taking another breath quite so deep.

Eerie night-sounds slithered, crept and crawled. He saw movement in the trees above. *But if it's night, how can I see anything? It should be black as pitch. My lantern*, he reasoned. *Yes.* He glanced sideways. The lamp sat a few feet away, its flame extinguished. An unexpected sound reached his ears—a voice, but he lacked the strength to turn his head.

* * *

Ceese's sprint to the door caught Brendan off guard, but he managed to grab her up at the last second. "You're not going anywhere!"

Ceese squirmed and pushed against the thick arm that held her. "Turn me loose."

"Not until you calm yourself."

Her small form stiffened in stubborn resistance. "Richard's in trouble. I have to go to him. I have to help him."

"I'm fairly certain he can take care of himself, little one. Anyway, he's just gone off to read last rites to a dying man."

15

She struggled even more. "Turn me loose, or I'll tell Father I saw you alone with Millie Parson—in this very room. I'll tell him that I saw you *kiss* her."

"Well, that would be a convenient lie, wouldn't it?"

"You were by the inglenook—the two of you—and you were holding hands. I saw you." She pointed with a stiff finger. "Right over there."

"That's a nice story, but you couldn't have seen anything because I made sure no one was around—" He sucked in air at the inadvertent slip of the tongue. "You tricked me into saying that, you little imp!"

"I'll tell Father what you just called me. He'll have your tongue."

Brendan's shoulders slumped at the possibility of having Father angry at him again. "All right, but if I put you down, you have to swear not to tell Father any of what you know."

"I swear it." As soon as her feet hit the floor, Ceese ran, straight away, back to the room where the girls slept and shut the door.

At least she's gone back to bed, Brendan thought, but the *whack* of a window thrown open suggested otherwise. He charged the shut door and, with some effort, threw it open, breaking the chair that held it in place. He lunged toward his sister, hoping to grab her before she escaped, but Ceese scrambled madly out of reach. Brendan climbed out behind her and gave chase

16

until he saw her enter the forest, a lit lantern swinging at her side.

He would have to get a lantern as well to follow her. He planted a heel to turn back toward the house but tensed at the sound of muted footfalls on soft earth behind him. Wild animals reacted badly to sudden movements, so he proceeded with caution.

Wolf-eyes met his. But this was no wolf. Not exactly anyway.

"Joachim?"

"I give you my oath that I'll protect her," the werewolf said, flawlessly impersonating Brendan and speaking the same words Brendan spoke to him six years ago. "I can take care of her. I will make certain nothing happens to her."

The impersonation drew Brendan's ire. "Don't do that. Don't parrot me." Joachim's uncanny, and unnerving, ability to mimic lost its appeal six years ago. And time hadn't changed that for Brendan.

But Joachim continued, this time using Father's voice and speaking in Gaelic. "It seems the boy has grown into a man, but I wonder if he has likewise grown in knowledge and wisdom."

The silvery light from the full moon brightened darker shadows, and Brendan stared uncertainly at Joachim. "What the devil are you wearing? Are those ladies' pantaloons?"

17

Joachim answered in his proper voice, his accent all over the place. He sounded much like a Scotsman at first, his words a bit sing-songy. Then, all at once, he sounded nothing like a Scotsman but more like a proper Englishman, biting off his words and sounding quite posh. "I took them from a line," he gestured over his shoulder, "up the road — still a wee bit on the soggy side. P'haps I should slog around in my all-together—?

"No, no!" Brendan rushed, waved his hands in front of him when Joachim made a move to disrobe. "That's all right. I appreciate your effort to cover yourself."

Brendan had another question, though. His eyes narrowed to dangerous slits. "Where were you a month ago? We had an intruder. And Richard mentioned seeing wolf eyes before being hit in the back of the head. Was that you?"

"I saved your brother that day at the river, didn't I? Makes no sense to assume I was the intruder that harmed him, now does it?"

"Who then? Was it the one you spoke of six years ago? The one responsible for Mother's attack?"

Joachim nodded. "He's come for her. He's come to fetch your sister."

"That means he's probably out there now. Ceese is out there too. I have to go after her." Brendan pushed past Joachim, entered the house, and came back with a lit lantern. "I could use your help."

"All right then," Joachim said, pointed. "She went that way."

"More help than that would be nice. How about you go get Ceese since you seem to know where to look?"

"Are you asking?"

"If you need my permission, then yes."

Brendan watched Joachim leave. Tried to push aside the feeling of dread associated with sending a known man-wolf off in search of his six-year-old sister.

* * *

Richard lay on the ground.

"Ye bloody well promised!" he heard someone say. "Ye can't renege on me now. Wot right 'ave ye got?"

The drifter. The man who'd shown up looking for Father. It was his voice. Richard told the man Father was not home and wasn't expected back until morning, which was truth. "But I can oblige you," Richard said to the stranger. Richard performed the act of reading last rites often, sometimes with Father's guidance and sometimes without. And the stranger told him his friend lay nearby. That meant he could return in plenty of time to continue preparations for his ordination the next day.

The drifter continued to rage. "I've done wot ye asked. Now ye'll bloody well come through with yer end of the ba'gain."

"But I've changed my mind," a woman's voice replied, a voice Richard recognized at once.

Jasmine. His betrothed. *How can it be—? She's visiting her mother.* The question flew from his mind, his too-tired-to-move body yanked up by a shoulder and into a sitting position. His head slumped forward; his neck strained from the weight of it.

"I've waited far too long for this," Jasmine cooed close to his ear. "Far too long. The more of his blood I take, the less effect *you'll* have until eventually, he's all mine." A tug-of-war began. Richard felt like a limp, hapless ragdoll pulled back and forth. Just as he lost consciousness, he heard a child's voice reciting in Gaelic. *"Arr NAH-hr uh thah air NEE-uv . . ."*

* * *

Seven-year-old Richard's heart pounded in his chest. Sweat beaded as he ran. A severe chill in the air that morning called for long sleeves. A branch snagged the fabric of one sleeve as he brushed by and tore a hole. Richard sucked in air. Mother would undoubtedly scold him about tearing his clothes, but what could he do about it now? To prevent more damage to the shirt, he pushed both sleeves up over his elbows and ran on. He ducked low branches, pulled and pushed through thick brush, then ran faster than he ever imagined he could. Briars tore at exposed skin, but at least his shirtsleeves would be spared.

Cyn No More

"Risiart! Cá bhfuil sibh?"

Wild-eyed, the boy stopped in his tracks, struck by the alarm in Father's voice, and at Father calling to him in Gaelic. He spun around slowly as the sound seemed to come from all around, but Father didn't call out again.

"I'm here," the boy replied, his breath coming in quick, short bursts. Getting no answer, he ran on; desperate to find his way out of the forest and to Father.

The afternoon sun continued its slide toward the horizon. Shadows stretched deceptively longer, shadows that hinted at a much darker something. A rotted log lay in the cover of one such shadow. Richard didn't see it in time and didn't react fast enough to leap over it. A solid thud marked his fall, and he let out a surprised *"Uhn!"*

He gasped again when pulled up by a hand that gripped his collar and turned him around. With pupils the size of saucers, he cried out, "Father?"

Merideth Porter dropped to one knee, his minister's Geneva gown forming a pool of black fabric around him. He pulled Richard close and held him there for a long moment. "I thought I'd lost you, Richard." At arm's length, he asked, "But why were you running from me?"

"I wasn't running from you, Father, I was running to you. You called to me."

21

Sue Dent

"*Risiart*, I would never call you into a place of danger." He squinted at their surroundings and added words that sounded alarmingly foreboding, "certainly not into these woods. You know this. And I've warned you time and time again about going into the forest, haven't I? Why would you disobey me?"

Richard wilted under the weight of the question. He stared at the ground. "But you did call to me. I swear it. I heard you."

Merideth cupped Richard's chin with a hand and gently raised his head to look at him. "It's all right. I understand. You thought you heard me calling your name. Stranger things have happened in these woods. But it must've been the wind playing tricks. I daresay many have been fooled by it. But we should be getting back. In my haste to run after you, I didn't think to pick up a lantern—"

Both heads jerked toward an unearthly cry. Merideth gulped alarm. "No," then again, "no." He stood, placed protective hands on Richard's shoulders, and spoke to the air around them. "You can't take him; I won't let you." And then to Richard when he noticed something that he hadn't seen a moment ago. "You're bleeding."

Merideth reached around and untied his preaching bands: two long rectangular pieces of cloth. He tore at the fabric and dropped down to a knee. Taking Richard's left arm, he wrapped the fabric around deep

Cyn No More

scratches left by thorns.

With knitted brows, Richard watched. *The scratches didn't bother Father seconds ago. Why do they bother him now?*

Speaking out loud once more, Merideth said, "I won't make it easy for you to find him. I won't!"

"Who, Father? Make it easy for who?"

"Not your concern," but the tight lines on his face betrayed his words. With fumbling fingers, Merideth finished securing the bands. "There. That should do. But we should go now." He scooped Richard up in his arms. "We can move more quickly if I—"

That cry again and this time much closer. Merideth's pupils dilated to pinpoints. "Pray, *Risiart!*" Father bolted into a full run carrying Richard along. Face stretched with fear, Richard did as Father said and recited the Lord's Prayer in Gaelic, the way Father had taught it to him. His voice hitched with each jarring step. *"Arr NAH-hr uh thah air NEE-uv, guh NOO-veech-ehr DAH-nyim ..."*

* * *

Ceese easily navigated the dark-as-pitch forest with her now flameless lantern. She sprinted along as though she could see and as though she knew these woods well. But she had never been beyond the line of trees that marked the very edge of the woods.

Joachim followed but hesitated when Ceese darted out into a clearing. He scented the air; two vampires—and something else. Alarmed, he gave up the chase and ran in the opposite direction.

The first swipe of Zade's clawed hand ripped through the skin on Joachim's back. The next swipe took more skin and sent him to the ground.

"Joachim not find girl," he growled in werewolf-third-person, the pack falling in around him.

His body seizing in pain, Joachim sucked in air. "It's too soon anyway—to take her. She would die. Still too young."

Zade dropped down on all fours. Joachim squeezed his eyes shut against the hot breath beating his face. "Joachim not tell Zade what to do. Joachim never tell Zade what to do. Joachim has forgotten his place in the pack. Joachim must learn."

Zade's jaw opened wide. Canine-like fangs threatened. Joachim scrambled to get his arms up in front of him. "U-u-uncle," he cried out. And then again, "uncle."

After a long moment, Zade relaxed his jaw. "Uncle," the werewolf repeated, angrily. "When that no longer matters, Joachim will feel the sting of death."

* * *

Cyn No More

Richard's eyes sprang open. But he wasn't seven anymore. Just recalling some distant happening. *But this is real*; the forest canopy looming overhead, night sounds all around, and the repugnant stench of a rotting carcass still far too close. Something different, though. Someone was smoothing his hair.

He recognized his six-year-old sister. "Ceese?"

His head in her small lap, her mouth formed an "O" and those hazel eyes rounded. "You're alive!"

This reaction from someone who, four short weeks ago, "wished him away forever?" At times her jealousy for Father's attention drove her to prank Richard. Often, she'd sneak a handful of crickets down the back of his shirt or yank at his hair without reason. Though she'd done none of these things since her change of heart, the night of the intruder, Richard worried none-the-less. Abruptly he sat up. A little too abruptly. He put a hand out to steady himself and waited for the forest to stop spinning.

Ceese moved to stand. "I thought they killed you. I don't want you to die."

Her nightgown, littered as it was with debris from the forest floor, let Richard know she had walked quite a way. "But how did you find me?"

"When that evil man came to fetch you, I followed."

"But I told Brendan to put you back to bed," *after you called the visitor evil, and loud enough so he could hear.*

She swatted wispy hair from her face. "I got back up after you left and ran for the door. Brendan grabbed me, but I told him I'd tell Father how I saw him alone with Millie Parsons if he didn't put me down. Then I pretended to go to bed but escaped out the bedroom window."

Less than a week ago, Father reprimanded Brendan for holding hands with Millie in public and promised punishment if he didn't work harder to curve his promiscuous behavior. "I see. And so, you followed me here then."

"Yes. I even brought a lantern." She pointed proudly to the now dark lamp on the ground. *It must've just gone out*, he reasoned, and the moon offered enough light for her to see now.

"But you being here—that means you saw what happened. You saw everything." Everything he couldn't recall. He moved from a sitting position and settled back on his heels. "Please tell me what happened, Ceese. Tell me what you saw."

She drew back from him. "I don't want to remember."

"But I need to know. I can't recall anything. Just tell me whatever it is you can bring yourself to say." To her shrinking away, he added, "Don't be afraid. Please, Ceese. It's important to me."

Cyn No More

"They fought over you," she hissed. "Th-they fought over you like a toy that they both wanted badly. Then they bit you." She pointed to the heart-shaped "angel kiss" birthmark on his neck, the one they both inherited from Mother. "Right there. You stopped moving after that." She balled her small hands into defiant fists. "That's when I stepped out and prayed. I prayed loudly."

"In Gaelic." Richard nodded. "The Lord's Prayer. I heard you just before I passed out."

"Yes. And they ran away, those two."

Nervous, he looked around. "Yes, well, perhaps we should go as well and before Father returns and finds out you're missing." *Or before those two come back for the both of us.*

"I'm sorry," Ceese said with conviction.

"Sorry about what? You saved my life."

"I'm sorry I ever wished you away. I didn't mean it." She lunged forward and threw her tiny arms around his neck. "Please forgive me."

"If it makes you feel better, then yes, I forgive you," he said. *So young. So vulnerable. I could so easily take her blood—* "No!" He held her at arm's length, forced through thoughts he couldn't believe he was having. "I mean *no* reason to hang around here any longer. I should take you—um I should take you home now." *What is this urgency to seek refuge before the sun rises?*

Ceese pulled away, stumbled backward over her feet.

"What is it? What's wrong?" From the caustic look on her face, something certainly upset her.

"Y—you," she stammered and pointed. "You've got pointy teeth. Y—you're like them."

For Ceese's sake, he fought against his blood lust long enough to appear normal. "I'm not like them now," he said after a short moment and showed her his teeth as proof. At first reluctant and then willing, she allowed him to pick her up.

Cradling her small form, and after only a few steps, Richard heard the soft sounds of her sleeping. Very near the house, she stirred. "We must tell Father," she said. "He'll know what to do. He'll be able to help you."

"No, we must never tell Father. He should never know what happened. And if you say anything or tell anyone about it, then the two you saw fighting over me, they will come after Father. Do you want that?" The sheer terror in her eyes told him that she understood. But he needed to be sure. "Now swear to me that you won't tell."

"I swear it," she said.

Still so very tired, she fell back to sleep. Once at the house, Richard wrapped her in his coat and placed her

28

just at the front door. He heard her whisper in Gaelic. "*Nos da iwch.*"

"And goodnight to you as well," he said in return, placed a palm to her forehead, helped her temporarily forget the nightmare she had just lived through, realizing this was something he could do. He then stood and rapped on the door before rushing off.

Brendan yanked it open and breathed relief when he saw Ceese. He gathered her up but frowned confusion at Ceese wrapped in Richard's coat. Where was Joachim? He stared off into the woods, but there was no sign of the werewolf. Not understanding, Brendan carried Ceese inside.

* * *

"You see, girl is safe," Tobias said gruffly to Joachim's back. "We go now, or Zade get suspicious."

His back streaked with the results of Zade's attack, Joachim sank to the ground. Tobias hoisted his friend up onto his shoulders, scented the air, and set off to find the pack.

* * *

An uneasy dawn broke. Merideth Porter sat at his son's desk, eyes glazed and unfocused. Numbly he fingered the preaching bands. At the feeling that unseen eyes watched, he returned them to their hiding place.

Chapter 1

Present Day England

THE SUN SLUMBERED BENEATH the eastern horizon covered by a thick blanket of fog. A seasoned herder drove his trip of goats from the paddock and toward the pasture. Around his neck hung a silver chain dangling a sizeable crucifix. Close to the road, he could barely make out the Renault delivery van on its monthly route. It seemed to be running late, though, delayed no doubt by the fog.

Fondly weaned on Saturday Morning Cartoons, the herder smiled at the scene; a fog-shrouded box-shaped van, its low beams cutting a hard path through the pre-dawn darkness, its dashboard lights casting the hunkered-over-the-steering-wheel driver in an eerie glow revealing what could easily be mistaken as an 'if it hadn't been for you meddling kids' scowl. For a split second, it was Saturday Morning again, and the herder welcomed the memory as he moved his goats along.

* * *

"Bollocks!" shouted the driver, the front right tire slamming through yet another pothole with a bone-jarring *thud*. "Lot of good it does to pay council taxes. Roads are still a bloody mess."

Cyn No More

He squinted through the smothering fog that pressed against the windshield like a tightly wrapped blanket. He gripped the steering wheel with both hands. Another pothole like that one could cost him an axle, and he had no desire to be stranded on this God-forsaken stretch of road where dead and bloodless livestock turned up in pastures where they grazed. At least that's what a recent copy of the *Sunday Sports* reported, a tabloid he regularly read.

"Vampires killed 'em and drank their blood," the paper quoted one victimized goat-herder as saying, and though the words read like crazy-talk, each dead animal did have a set of identical puncture wounds on the neck. "They live in that castle." A photograph accompanied the article. "I've seen 'em. Nothing like this happened before *they* moved in." The goat herder's words stuck with the courier like a festering splinter in his mind. It didn't help that his route would take him to the very castle mentioned in the article.

Distracted and with the fog so thick, the courier easily missed subtle hints that marked the grand curve in the road. He jerked the steering wheel hard one way and then back in the opposite direction dodging trees on the right and avoiding a deep rocky ravine to his left. He came out of the curve without incident, and the fog gave up a little of its thickness.

Up ahead, the castle floated in the murky white landscape. The crown of each stone turret glowed from lights installed at the last renovation and seemed to hover above their fog-shrouded base resembling every B-movie UFO he'd ever seen.

Upon passing the main structure, a grand downstairs window filled with light. A large man wearing a dark coat stood on the other side, staring out. *What's this?* He had never seen anyone other than the elderly Ms. Penelope on previous deliveries. He thought about this as he made the turn into the driveway that ran along the southeast end of the castle and parked.

* * *

Brendan Porter, his thick beard shaved, stared out the large parlor window and squinted from beneath thick brows at the bright headlights of the passing van. He was still wearing his long duster with its arm-less left sleeve tucked in a pocket as well as his holstered pistol-gripped, sawed-off shotgun hanging from his hip and strapped to his right leg.

"Aye, seems we've a guest," he said in thick Scottish brogue.

Penny directed her gaze over his shoulder. "It's just the courier. Richard's monthly delivery of blood. I guess we won't be needing that anymore." She turned back to face the small group behind her. A wheelchair tucked away in a nook caught her attention; a simple reminder that less than two weeks ago, her childhood friend Ceese, a werewolf at the time, reversed her physical age by some thirty years.

"What do you mean you heard Rodney's thoughts?"

Cyn No More

Penny heard her granddaughter say to Ceese; the century-old teen stuck at age eighteen for most of her life. "I understand that a werewolf can 'sense' what others think—but how could you possibly do that if you're no longer cursed?"

"I wasn't talking to you," the ex-werewolf rebutted, her tone resentful and cold.

"Ceese," Penny admonished. "You promised you'd try harder to get along with Cassie. And Cassie, "I'm sure Ceese didn't mean to say she could *hear* Rodney's thoughts. She probably just meant that she knows Rodney well enough to believe that he'll help find Joachim. Isn't that right, dear?"

"If you say so," came Ceese's attempt at civility.

Penny frowned at her banal reply.

"Hold up," Rodney said, waved his hands in front of him, the longer neon blonde bangs of his two-tone hair, blond and jet black, partially falling across one eye where he let it stay. "No way am I going to help hunt werewolves anymore. This Joachim," he said to Ceese, "he's a werewolf, right?"

"Yes. Now that Zade is gone, he'll come back as one. That is—if Brendan is right and Joachim didn't curse anyone before he died."

"Yeah, well, I'm sorry, but if I see another werewolf, I'm heading the other way."

Rodney's abrasive friend, Kyle, who arrived a day

ago with the DNA test results Rodney requested, enthusiastically whipped his cell phone from a pant pocket. "Finally, you're making sense." He moved his finger around the screen of his phone. "I'll just pull up the app and make reservations for the next flight back to New York."

Rodney squinted at Kyle. "What side of stupid did you wake up on?"

"How can you wake up when you've had no sleep," Kyle snapped. "I've been up all night chasing werewolves and stepping in bear dung, remember?"

"Well, I didn't say anything about going home yet. Josh is still a vampire. I'm here for him, you know, to help him temper his bloodlust, so he doesn't feed on us. But you're free to go whenever."

Brendan shouted from where he stood at the window, "Would ye please shut it? I've had enough of this idle chit-chat, and what the devil's taking Brother so long? What does Father have to say to him that he cannae say to us all? Why send us all down here to the parlor to wait?"

Penny tried to sound hopeful. "I'm sure we'll find out soon enough."

Chapter 2

IN A REMOTE PASTURE not far from the castle and not long after dawn broke, dirt rushed across the ground with no wind to drive it and nothing else to explain its movement; a horizontal avalanche of soil that came together and piled up to form a single mound approximately three feet high and roughly seven feet in length. A herd of unattended goats grazed nearby. Several ventured close to nibble at the grasses that poked through loose dirt around the very edges. All at once, and with all the surprise of a Jack-in-the-Box springing out, a sinewy arm punched through the side and showered earth all around. A hand at the end of it grabbed the closest goat by the scruff and held tight until it fell limp. The owner of the appendage broke out of the dirt bank and sank its canine-like fangs into the animal's jugular, drawing a final bleat.

* * *

The courier moved around to the far side of the van, slid the side door open, and removed an insulated box marked "HUMAN BLOOD" from a refrigerated unit. He tossed his clipboard on top of the box and hip-bumped the door shut. An uneasy feeling swept over him at a round of wolf howls that split the silent predawn darkness. The hairs on the back of his neck prickled. He shuffled quickly up three short steps to knock on a door lit by a sidelight. A man answered, but not Ms. Penelope. The courier stared at the butler. "I have a delivery. Is the uh—Misses available." He hoped the delay in finding her wouldn't take long, the howls far too close for him to feel comfortable standing around in wait.

"I can sign for the package. If you look at your delivery instructions, you should see that I'm authorized to do so."

The courier glanced down and saw that the butler was correct. "Sorry 'bout that." Another round of howls left him all jittery. "J—just thought—uh, well, you know—sorry." He held out the clipboard for the butler to sign and then handed the package over. His obligation as courier fulfilled, he scurried back to the van, utilized the wide concrete parking pad at the end of the drive to turn, and sped off. The butler took the package inside.

* * *

In the forest that surrounded the castle, a man in a tweed jacket limp-ran through thick foliage. He dodged trees and leaped over obstacles in his path. At a barrier fence designed to keep livestock away from the road, he launched himself over, landing hard. His lame leg crumbled beneath him. He scrambled back to standing at the faint glow of day on the eastern horizon

Cyn No More

and ran on.

* * *

Spooked by the howling wolves and not able to forget the story about goat feeding vampires, the courier drove faster than the posted speed limit and raced along in spite of less than optimal visibility and slick roads, only slowing over creek beds and in low-lying areas where the fog held onto its thickness.

The headlights of the delivery van bounced off red reflectors affixed to guardrails up ahead. A fog bank hid the bridge beyond, but the courier knew this section of the road well. He sped across without slowing. When the van broke through the fog bank on the other side, the courier's chest tightened in terror. Something—no, *someone* had landed in the middle of his lane; a man in a tweed jacket who straightened and stretched his eyes wide at the sight of the van speeding toward him.

The courier stomped on the brake pedal. The van went into a skid. Turning the steering wheel hard, he managed to regain traction, but it was too late. A sickening thud marked the moment of impact just before the van came to a halt.

The courier loosened his white-knuckled grip on the steering wheel and fixated on the unconscious body in the road, barely visible over the hood. He closed his eyes against what he saw and muttered under his breath. "Please don't be dead. Please don't be dead."

Slitting his eyes, he peeked out.

The body was gone.

Relief washed over him. Perhaps the man was only injured. He used his cell to dial for Emergency Services.

"Nine, nine, nine," a voice squawked, "what service?"

Before the courier could respond, the driver's side door yanked open. A hand grabbed his phone and threw it."

"What service?" he heard the voice repeat as the cell flew into the air.

Blinking fear at tweed-jacket man's razor-sharp fangs, the courier shouted out, "*Vampire!*"

* * *

From one of the two coffins in the castle's basement, a voice cried out, "No! Let him go."

Chapter 3

RICHARD OPENED HIS EYES and pushed up from the floor. With a lost look and quite a bit of wobble to his step, he entered the hall and headed downstairs.

* * *

Distinctive white hair meticulously combed, his livery pressed and creased, Richard's butler from years past, and recently re-hired, carried an arm full of clean towels. He stopped briefly to direct a servant to another task when he saw his employer stagger down the hall toward the parlor, his pallor unnaturally ashen, his left hand pressed against his neck. Geoffrey thrust the towels at the servant in front of him. "Take these to the washroom upstairs for me," he said in flawless Queen's English. "I have an urgent matter to attend to."

* * *

Vampire? It can't be.

No matter how hard she tried, Penny could not deny, as she stood with the others in the parlor, that Richard had that look. Penny stared after Richard as he stumbled and grabbed the open door for support. She rushed to his side to steady him.

Sue Dent

"What on earth? Richard, you look as though you've seen a ghost." She wiped at his shoulder, hoping not to see evidence of her suspicions. Her eyes slowly walked up to his neck, and she whispered, "It … it's blood."

Her next words lodged in her throat at seeing a set of puncture wounds. Then there was the oddly familiar harshness that now marked, and had marked, his features in the not-so-distant past. Also, his pale-blond hair hung loose instead of being pulled back and tied, a look he preferred since his return from New York—free of the vampire's curse.

Penny stared, and Richard returned her stare, seeing but not seeing. In an instant of recognition, the anonymity lifted.

"Mamá."

Her eyes rounded at hearing the pet name he had given her so that outsiders had an acceptable reason as to why an elderly woman might be living alone with a much younger man; a name he hadn't called her since he'd gotten back from New York. He pulled away from the door frame to stand on his own.

"Are you all right?" Penny asked.

He slipped his hands in his pockets and feigned composure. "I … I'm not sure what you're talking about."

His words were truth Penny knew, a troubling truth.

Cyn No More

If Richard were indeed a vampire again, as the fresh bite marks, along with his no-longer-bound up hair, and his calling her *Mamá* suggested, he wouldn't be able to answer the most basic question about himself. Penny's own experience as a vampire told her the amnesia of those freshly turned could last for a while, depending on the individual and the situation.

He glared fiercely at those standing around. "Who are these people?"

His eyes fell on Cassie, who, in turn, cut her eyes toward Penny as if to say, 'what's going on.' Penny returned a glance that suggested caution.

Cassie fixed evermore-dubious eyes on Richard. "You don't know who we are or who I am?"

"I'm quite certain my words were clear," he said. "In fact, I've lived in this castle for the better half of a centur—" he quickly reworded as if to avoid suspicion. "Uh, *years*. And I can honestly say I've never seen any of you around."

The corner of Cassie's mouth tightened. This time she glanced over at Penny to seek understanding. Penny shrugged in return.

Richard monitored the silent exchange with a scrutinizing eye. "Are you two hiding something from me?" Then to Penny directly, "And are you doing something different with your hair? You look dramatically, younger. I dare say *much* younger than you did the last time I saw you."

41

Penny chose her words carefully. "Richard, Ceese gave me some of my youth back. Surely you recall that."

She wondered from his long pause if she had said too much or pushed too hard. It certainly wouldn't be helpful to have him fly into a rage now as most vampires were prone to do when they didn't understand. She breathed relief when his gaze fell on Ceese: with recognition.

"Did she now?" he said, fishing through jumbled memories. "Gave you back some of your youth. What a nice gesture, I suppose. Especially since she's usually not so easy to get along with."

He moved to glare at the others in turn. "But are we having a party? You must know how I detest parties."

"We're not having a party, Richard. The people you see were all invited by you to stay here."

"Really, Mamá? I'm growing weary of this game you're playing with me. Why would I invite total strangers into my home?"

That sealed it in Penny's mind. His tone, his arrogance, this was the rebellious vampire she'd been living with for nearly a century, not the mortal who'd returned to the castle from New York less than a week ago.

Something else struck her: an all-too-familiar emotion, a *strong* emotion, this was the Richard she loved and not the man she told Cassie she no longer felt for romantically.

Chapter 4

RICHARD TOOK MEASURED STEPS into the parlor. "What about the goat herder, I believe Drummond is his name? I'm assuming he took the cash I offered him for his missing goats," he cut his eyes to target Ceese, "even for the ones that I did not take. Was that enough to satisfy him?"

"Yes," Penny said, hoping that her expression alone was enough to convince Ceese not to speak on the matter despite her knowing more. Ceese remained silent.

Richard approached his outsized mahogany desk and slowed his pace. He glanced at the clutter atop it, seeing but not understanding.

"Those things were from our planning session last night," Penny gently prodded. "The antique balancing piece, the nautical charts ..."

"Of course, they are," he snapped back, agitated as he moved on, continuing to notice things but at the same time not notice them. A particular throw rug seemed to catch his attention.

"Ceese did a wonderful job repairing that, did she not?" Penny asked. "Cutting away the burned area.

Cyn No More

Why you can hardly tell …"

Richard walked on. He dismissed Cassie's prone-to-be obnoxious roommate Rodney and his equally intolerable partner in crime, Kyle, as strangers. He offered Brendan a curious stare and eventually stopped with his back to the parlor's three large windows.

The windows faced east. Time ticked by. A faint glow hinted at daybreak, and within those scant seconds, the first rays of sun stabbed their way through a line of trees at the edge of the lawn.

From his vantage, Rodney saw wispy white smoke as it curled out from Richard's left pant leg. He shared what he saw by belting out a line from a pop-song, chart-topper. Right on pitch, he sang, *That man is on fi-yer.*"

To Richard's confused look, he added, nodding toward the smoke. "Seriously, dude, you're on fire."

Richard followed Rodney's gaze and gasped. As though struck with a cattle prod, he bolted forward and dove over a nearby sofa to safety. A solid thud marked his landing. On his back, he slid his pant leg up and patted away flame. To the faces that now looked down at him, he said indignantly, "What right did *any* of you have to leave my drapes open? Invited or not, go home."

"You left the drapes open, Richard," Penny told him.

"That's right," Cassie said next. "You said you liked them like that now that you're no longer a—" Penny's caustic look made Cassie shift course "—I mean, now that you're back from New York."

No longer sporting flames, Richard propped himself up on his elbows. "That's preposterous! I've never been to New York, at least not lately. And I would never make such a request."

"Aye, have ye taken leave of yer senses, brother?"

Richard pulled his head back in shock. "Brother?" he spat out. "Who the devil—" He glared at Penny, "Mamá, are you taking in vagrants again? Must you really? And he only has one arm. He won't even make a good servant."

Ceese squinted confusion. "You don't know who Brendan is?"

"No, I don't know who *Brendan* is, but I know who you are. You broke my computer's mouse. You burned my rug, and you shredded my lamb's wool bathrobe."

Ceese scowled. "I fixed your mouse *and* your rug, and I did not shred your bathrobe. The wolf did. It smelled of sheep."

"Wolf or not, you still owe me for that bathrobe. And why are you still here? Why aren't you with that—that werewolf friend of yours? What's his name, Zane—Zade? He seems to like you an awful lot. Much better than I do."

Cyn No More

Kyle, a definitive Curly to Rodney's Mo, smirked sarcastically and said, "didn't you get the memo? Ceese isn't a werewolf anymore. But of course, you know that, because you were with her in New York when her curse was lifted. And *you* were the one who threw the knife with your dad's vampire blood on it to rescue Ceese from Zade. You know—the knife of the '*Akedah*' or whatever it is everybody keeps calling it. You nailed him with those bizarre circus-knife-throwing skills of yours." Kyle emulated the toss with the flick of his wrist. "Bullseye!"

Richard turned to glare at Kyle; his tightly curled shock of red hair, his multiple facial piercings, tattoos, and dryly replied as though he hadn't heard anything the punk had said. "Is it Halloween, or perhaps some other costumed holiday that I'm not aware of?"

Penny closed her eyes and sighed.

Chapter 5

"DON'T LOOK AT ME like that," Penny said to the stares her sigh brought. She relaxed when Geoffrey entered the parlor taking the group's attention off her. The butler went to the window and drew the drapes at once. He walked over to where Richard lay behind the couch.

"I have a blanket to cover you with, sir," he said, "so you can make it to your basement without further incident."

"Finally, someone I recognize. Geoffrey, please tell me my eyes aren't deceiving me."

Geoffrey knelt to arrange the blanket. "I saw you in the hall a moment ago, your hand against your neck. I suspected something might be different."

"Then, my eyes aren't deceiving me." Bewilderment crossed his features. "Yet, I don't recall hiring you back on."

"Of course, you don't recall, but let's get you to your coffin, nonetheless. The explanation can wait until after you've rested."

"I'm certainly very tired. Not to mention charred." Richard glared at those he felt responsible when he

Cyn No More

said this.

"Indeed, you should be tired," Geoffrey replied. "This is your time to rest."

Geoffrey helped Richard to stand then ushered him along, parting those who stood around as eloquently as Charlton Heston parted the cinematic red sea in 'The Ten Commandments.' Just before stepping out into the hall, Richard peeked out from his blanket and announced in a voice that could be heard by all, "Whoever left my drapes open will pay. Geoffrey, I want you to deal with the ones responsible. I want them punished. Do you understand? Let the punishment fit the crime."

Geoffrey gave his employer the slightest lifting of an eyebrow. "Shall we hang them from the highest tree, then?"

"Indeed. Let's do that. Set them atop our best stallion and make certain I'm there to spur the horse on so I can watch the perpetrator swing lifeless once they've dropped."

In the hall, Richard lowered his voice as he and the butler walked. "Do you suppose they took me seriously?"

"Doubtful. Unless they aren't aware that you have no stable, nor do you have any stallions."

"I don't?"

"No m'lord. You never really fancied horses, nor

did you ever have time for them."

"How could I have forgotten that?"

"It's not all that unusual." At the entrance to the basement, Geoffrey opened the door and led the way down the stairs. At the bottom, he pointed to a side table. "I have a warmed pouch of blood for you there." The pouch sat on a saucer atop a silver tray as though it deserved such treatment.

Richard looked where Geoffrey pointed. "What would I do without you, man? I don't even care that I don't recall exactly how you came to be in my service again after so many years." He stopped and smiled slightly. "Wait. Some of it's coming back to me. Your father—he's a vampire. That's why I hired you in the first place because you had experience. Did you ever find him, your father, I mean? I recall you were looking."

"No, I have yet to find him, but thank you for asking."

"Yes, of course. But why wouldn't I ask? We're very close like that, aren't we?"

"I'd like to think so."

"I'd like to remember so. Though, I can't seem to recall much of anything."

"It will come back to you soon enough. Perhaps things will move along faster this time around."

Cyn No More

Richard turned to stare at the butler. "This time around—Geoffrey ... man, if you know something, please share."

"Anything I can tell you will only stand to confuse you more at the moment. I will say that things should make more sense after you've had a good day's rest."

Richard nodded appreciatively. "At the very least, I can put stock in your words."

"Implicitly, I would never lie to you."

Richard cut his eyes to the right. "Why are there two coffins instead of just the one?"

The shape of his memory was too fragile to bother explaining. The information that Rodney's drug-addicted-friend-turned-vampire occupied the second coffin would only confuse him more presently.

"Let's just let that be a mystery for now." Geoffrey reached inside a front pocket of his shirt and removed an elastic band. "Shall I bind your hair up for the day, or would you prefer to do it yourself?"

"Yes, I do like my hair bound up while I rest, don't I." Richard turned his back to the butler, "If you could."

Geoffrey reached out, smoothed the longer part of Richard's hair with a brush from the same tray that held the blood pouch, and then eased in the band. "If that's all m'lord, I shall leave you to your breakfast and your coffin."

"There is one thing," Richard said.

"Yes."

"I suppose that *um* … that I'd like to thank you for something, for everything."

"No need," Geoffrey reminded, with the slightest hint of a smile. "As always, your thanks are understood. Rest well."

* * *

In ethereal form, it hovered close to the exposed joists that supported the castle's main floor. The *daoine maithe*, believed by some to be fallen angels and by others to be the figments of a drunken imagination, worked tirelessly and against their will to facilitate its physical to ethereal transformation.

Footfalls below brushed the wooden steps that led down into the basement. Since it could see and hear, it watched and listened. The butler and his employer conversed as they walked and then stopped by a small table. After a few words, the butler took a hairbrush from a tray, gathered the length of his employer's hair, and bound it up.

It sighed longingly. *Oh, to be the one holding that brush. To be so near—*

The employer abruptly turned his head. "Did you hear that?"

Had it made a noise? Could it? Though it could hear

and see in its new form, it wasn't aware that anyone could hear or see it.

"I suspect it was the castle, sir. Lots of sounds here in the basement, from the weight of it bearing down."

The employer didn't question the explanation, and the butler left shortly afterward. The employer then headed off with a pouch of blood on which to feed.

* * *

For the most part, vampires preferred to feed in private. Therefore, Richard sought out and found a suitable crawl space; one that afforded him a lookout. He raised the blood pouch to his lips and struck the bag with razor-sharp fangs. Once sated, and the bag empty, he returned it to the tray and made the short walk back to his coffin. Settled inside, he reached up to ease the lid down but froze with it midway open.

Vampire bats! That's why it's important to feed before I rest. And to rest in an airtight coffin, so the vampire's lure doesn't have a chance to draw in vampire bats instead of a quick meal.

There was nothing worse than waking up with a horde of thumb-sized varmints attached and suckling. Richard shuddered at that thought and eased the coffin's lid down the rest of the way.

Chapter 6

"WHY SHOULDN'T WE LOOK to ye for answers?" Brendan all but shouted at Penny, the long tail of his duster flaring out as he spun to face her. "It seems he recalls ye with ease."

Penny remained calm in spite of the large man's harsh tone and his intimidating nature. She'd seen his softer side when he reminisced and spoke of his beloved Gwen.

"He recalled Ceese as well," she pointed out.

"Aye, but only the way she was as a werewolf."

"Yes," Cassie said, her disenchantment coming through in her tone, the kiss she and Richard shared in the hallway of the ER, the one in her bedroom; both memories grew more and more distant.

An empathetic Penny said, "I'm sorry, Cassie. I know it must be difficult for you. Believe me. I know what it's like to lose Richard—" her voice hitched. She looked away as though to hide something and then turned back more composed.

Cyn No More

"I mean to have Richard not know who you are."

"Well, I'm glad he doesn't know who I am," Kyle confessed, rubbed at his neck with a hand, "especially since he seems to be a vampire again."

"But it nae makes sense," Brendan frowned. "Who would want to curse him?"

"Do we know for sure that Josh went back to his coffin?" Cassie asked.

Rodney shot her a hard look. "Why wouldn't he have gone to his coffin? That's where he said he was going."

"You don't need to get defensive. I'm just asking. I mean, we did bring Josh to Richard's estate so Richard could help him temper his desire for blood because of his addiction issue. And no one knows for sure whether he fed earlier—before he brought Meri back to the castle."

"What about Henderson?" Kyle challenged, bringing up the college professor who successfully cursed himself by self-injecting vampire stem cells he had harvested from animals on which Richard fed. "He cursed Josh. And he was out in the forest with us last night. Why aren't we considering him?"

"Excellent point," Rodney commended, raising

55

a clenched hand, rewarding Kyle with a rare fist-bump.

"I'm sorry to cut your celebration short," Geoffrey said, returning to tidy up from last night's planning session. "I did see someone resembling Master Josh in the hall earlier."

"With all the servants around here," Kyle said, "it could've been anybody." Kyle geared up for another fist-bump, but Rodney left him hanging.

"There's no mistaking Josh for someone else. Not with those dreads of his. If G-man says he saw him, then he probably did."

Cassie rolled her eyes at hearing Rodney use the moniker he assigned the butler when they first arrived at the castle from New York.

"I'm sorry," Geoffrey replied. "I wish I had seen someone else."

Brendan glowered, took slow steps over to Rodney. Green penetrating eyes focused, and jaw clenched, he said, "He best nae be the one."

Ceese moved in between the two and faced Brendan. "Leave him alone. He can't control what Josh does."

"Why do ye do that?" Brendan snarled. "Why do ye protect him? Let him fight his own battles."

Cyn No More

Penny tried her best to maintain a modicum of control. "Look. We don't know that Josh did anything. We're just looking for answers."

"Which seems to include ignoring the obvious," Rodney said. "Why is no one considering 'Daddy Dearest'—you know, Meri? He's a vampire too. And he asked to be alone with Richard sending the rest of us down here to the parlor."

"Yes," Brendan defended in a loud voice, "so they could talk."

"He hadn't fed since he lost all that blood from being stabbed," Rodney fired back. "*And* he hadn't touched either one of the two pouches of blood we took to him. How do you think that conversation went?"

"He wouldnae curse, Richard."

Stumbling footfalls overhead drew their attention to the ceiling. "That's coming from Meri's room," Penny said, knowing the layout of the castle well.

* * *

Tweed-jacket-man, chased by the sun's rays, rushed the entrance of the cave, tripped on an exposed root, and fell palms down in the remnants of a smoldering campfire from the evening before.

Sue Dent

He pushed up in response to the searing pain and quickly brushed hot embers off on a pant leg even as he sprinted the short distance to the cave's mouth, dove head-first, and scrambled along the dirt floor. He located the nearest dark crevice and crawled inside, the need to rest, hitting him like a hammer. He stripped off his tweed jacket and balled it up into a makeshift pillow just in time for it to softly catch his head.

Chapter 7

MERIDETH PORTER STUMBLED AROUND like someone trying to find their sea legs. His mind a blank, he struggled to recall anything. The chair by his bed sparked a memory.

"Richard," he whispered aloud. *Richard sat there while we talked, expressed his concern over having to stab me to coat the knife's blade with my blood.*

Meri put a hand on the soaked bandage that covered the wound. Something was different, though. Very different. He pulled at the tape that held the dressing in place and inhaled sharply at the smooth, healed skin revealed.

He rushed the wardrobe on the other side of the room, yanked open its mirrored doors.

"What's this?" he said of his reflection. Brown eyes stared back at him — Richard's eyes. Perfect lips smiled — Richard's smile. His image reminded him so much of his eldest son, his near-twin, that he choked back emotion. Tracing his reflection with shaky fingers, he said, "I've not seen you in forever."

Footfalls echoed in the hall. Quickly, he grabbed a clean shirt and shoved his arms into it.

Sue Dent

* * *

They left the parlor as a group. Brendan led the way, down the hall and up the stairs. Then just as Brendan prepared to knock on the closed door, it opened.

The shock of recognition—of Meri standing there looking well, rendered Brendan speechless. When he found his voice, he said, "We heard noises." And then, without any invitation at all, he walked in, followed by the others. Six sets of confused eyes turned to stare at Meri and then past him.

In his rush, he had left the wardrobe doors open. The mirror became the focus of attention. "Oh that," he said of his reflection. "I can explain."

Their stunned expressions told him he should—and right away. "We're listening," Cassie said, not giving much away in her tone.

His explanation didn't come fast enough for Penny, though, and a curtain of restraint held up by hopes of quick answers came crashing down.

"Richard's a vampire again, and you have a reflection. What did you do?"

Brendan stepped over to a bedside table. Held up one of two untouched pouches of blood and said, "Nary a drop drawn here yet ye look as if ye've feasted."

Rodney bent at the waist and picked something up

from the floor. "You didn't need this anymore?" He dangled a discarded bandage.

"I know what this must look like," Meri said, "but I assure you that everything—*everything* can be explained."

Brendan walked across the room and stopped in front of Meri. "Unbutton ye shirt. I want to see what ye're hiding."

"Nothing," Meri said calmly, slow fingers working at each button.

The last button unfastened, Brendan, reached out and eased the shirt open. "Aye, nary a mark. Nae even a scar. What indeed have ye done?"

Was that regret that flickered across his face like a flame dying out? Penny wondered. "How could you? You showed up here less than a week ago saying you wanted to help Richard and Ceese. How could you curse Richard again? I only let you stay here because I believed your words—believed *you*. I never sensed that you planned to harm your son."

"Exactly," Meri rallied, capitalizing on her words. "And that's significant because you're a seer and you can do that. You can sense those sorts of things. If you trust your ability as I know you do, then you know I had no plans of hurting Richard. None whatsoever, otherwise you would have known."

"Ye say ye never planned to harm Richard,"

Brendan said, "and I, for one, want to believe ye. But ye've nae touched the blood we left with ye, and ye asked for Richard to stay behind while ye sent the rest of us back to the parlor. Now the knife wound is gone—completely healed." He shook his head back and forth. "Say what ye will, but this very much has the look and feel of a plan to me. And nae a good one either."

A nervous Kyle chirped his fears. "Maybe he's still a vampire and just waiting for one of us to get close enough so he can get *more* blood!"

Meri directed everyone's attention back to the wardrobe's mirror. "You see my reflection."

Penny temporarily pursued Kyle's paranoid-driven line of logic for the sake of getting more information. "Vampires can fake being mortal long enough to lure in a victim. I know this from experience, and you know it as well."

A hapless laugh fell from Meri's lips, and he held his hands out in resignation as if to say, 'what's this,' but instead replied with, "So that's it, then. No one believes me, and it seems no one's going to believe me no matter what I say."

Ceese broke from her stupor at seeing the knife wound healed and at seeing Father's reflection. She pushed through the others and came to stand in front of him.

Chapter 8

"*Ciod E Dia?*"

Huh," Rodney grunted. "Was that English? Because it didn't sound like English."

"It's Gaelic," Brendan replied. "She asked him, 'What is God?'"

The corners of Meri's mouth curved up into a smile. "*Tha Dia na Spiorad. Neo-chriochnach, bith-bhuan, agus neo-chaochluidheach nabhith, na ghliocas, na chumhachd, na naomhachd, na cheartas, na mhaitheas, agus na fhìrinn.*"

"Okay," Rodney said, drawing out the word. "So, what did *he* say?"

Eyes glossed over with a thin sheen; Brendan translated. "God is a Spirit. Infinite, eternal, and unchangeable, in his being, wisdom, power, holiness, justice, goodness, and truth."

"A catechism," Penny nodded.

"A cata—what?" Rodney questioned.

Kyle answered in Penny's stead spitting out what he learned in *Religions in World Cultures 101* two

63

semesters past, the answer to the last question on an abhorrently long final exam. "A series of questions and answers used to explain the basic principles of a particular religion. More specifically, if your parents are Catholic, it's an extra hour of 'school' every Sunday where you're taught various and incredibly boring things about Catholicism."

Penny frowned slightly. "Catechisms are the foundation of many religions. A series of questions and answers, not specific to Catholics, that help teach the fundamentals."

"Aye, ye used to teach us in this manner," Brendan said to Father. "And it'd be near impossible for ye to think the words you just spoke, much less say them if ye still bore the vampire's curse."

"Fair enough," Penny said to Meri. "But Richard was with you before he showed up in the parlor—with bite marks on his neck. Now it seems that he's a vampire again and you aren't? And there are still two *full* units of blood on the nightstand. So, the question remains. What did you do?"

Calm, despite the accusations, Meri replied. "What I had to do. I had to save Richard from Cyn." Their bewildered expressions told him he needed to say more. "Not 'sin' as in 'go and sin no more.' Cyn as in short for Cynthia."

Kyle's face contorted into a mask of lines. "Go and '*C-Y-N*' no more? Yeah, like that makes more sense.

Cyn No More

Is anyone else as confused as I am?"

Penny ignored Kyle's obtuse, rambling this time as it was easier than paying attention to him. "You're going to have to do better than that, Meri."

As though pondering, Cassie repeated the name. "Cyn."

Meri's voice lifted at the prospect that Cassie might have heard of her. "Richard mentioned her to you?"

"He brought the name up the other night when he came to my room and—" Abruptly, she stopped talking. Why should she reveal something that she'd rather not disclose? She wasn't the one under interrogation. Her cheeks blushed red recalling the intimate moment she and Richard shared, and she pushed a strand of auburn hair behind an ear. With guarded words, she finished her sentence. "—when he'd come to talk."

"What did he tell you about her?" Meri eagerly prodded, "—about Cyn?"

"He just mentioned her. That's all." Because of her inability to lie with ease, Cassie hoped the questions would stop.

"Who is Cyn?" Penny blurted as though bothered by what she didn't know. "I've never heard the name, and I've lived with Richard for nearly a century."

"She's one of the two who cursed him," Meri replied.

"I've talked with Richard numerous times before, about that very thing. The names he gave, the few times he could bring himself to discuss the ordeal, were Tristan and Jasmine."

"Jasmine?" Brendan questioned. "Richard's betrothed?"

"Richard's betrothed?" Cassie echoed. "You mean he's engaged?"

"Engaged?" Penny said, rattled. "I'm fairly certain I'd know if he were engaged or ever had been."

"Well, it was hardly an engagement that he agreed to," Meri said, ending the volley of questions. "Cyn— or rather Jasmine as she called herself at the time, tricked him and the rest of us. None of us knew who, or even what she was until it was too late to do anything about it."

"I knew," Ceese said. "I tried to tell all of you."

Meri, visibly shaken by this admission, replied with remorse in his voice. "We should've listened. Maybe things would've been different."

Brendan quickly came to Father's defense. "Aye, but Ceese was only six at the time and well known for temper-tantrums and getting her way. Sulking about and calling someone evil—that be her nature then."

"Would've, could've," Penny said, "I doubt having regrets about it now is going to help change anything presently. The past is the past. This vampire truly

Cyn No More

wanted Richard more than anything else. But how did Richard survive being cursed as I'm certain his soul was accounted for?"

Meri looked away. "He hadn't made it official. He wanted to wait until he was certain. He respected the commitment that much."

"Well, when you put it that way," Penny said, "I suppose it makes sense. That sounds very much like Richard."

"I learned later that Cyn wanted to take Richard as close to his ordination into the ministry as possible." Meri flinched at the pain the memory brought back; a pain not easy to forget. "She and Tristan claimed him on the eve before the day, as the blood of one so close to being 'off-limits' is said to be the most desirable. Richard disappeared that night, and I'd all but given up hope of ever finding him until quite a few years later when Cyn approached me with a proposal. It was her idea to fake my death." He paused before continuing. "You see, I was devastated by Richard's disappearance, Brendan can tell you this."

"Aye, ye grieved until ye passed," Brendan said, sad eyes hinting at the pain of watching Father mourn. "Or at least until we thought ye passed. And then *we* grieved, nae only for ye're passing but for Mother's as well." Brendan continued despite Father's stunned expression. "She could nae see her way to go on without ye. They said she passed from grief. That's all

67

that could explain it. And now," Brendan said, resentment slipping into his tone, "now ye say ye *faked* yer death? Ye had to know what it would do to Mother. Ye had to."

"I'm sorry. But you have to understand, Bren. I had to find Richard."

"Don't," Ceese said, looked all at once guilty of some horrible thing. "No one would be talking about any of this if I had just told what happened to Richard in the first place … if I had just said something."

"How could you know what happened?" Meri said. "None of us knew."

"When that man came by the house looking for someone to read last rites to his friend—I paid attention. He was lying. That wasn't what he wanted at all. After Richard left with him, I followed, and I saw everything."

Meri dismissed her words with a shake of his head. "But you were only six. No one would've let you go out after Richard. I'm sure of it."

"Richard put Brendan in charge when he left."

Recalling Brendan's impetuous youthful nature, Meri said, "I see."

"Aye, ye're going to look at me like that, are ye? After all this time. As if I nae changed."

"He did try to stop me," Ceese said, "but I

threatened to tell that I'd seen him kiss Millie Parsons—"

Brendan cut his eyes. "Ye aren't helping my case. And even at that, how can ye recall what happened that night with such clarity? That was nearly two centuries ago."

"I will never forget that night. I will never forget what I saw. Still, I have nightmares."

"If you did know," Meri said, "then why *did* you keep your silence, Cee Cee? Especially if it burdened you so?"

"Richard swore me to secrecy, and you taught us never to betray a trust. When I was older—as old as I am now, I set out looking for Richard on my own. Zade found me instead."

"Aye, the *blasted* werewolf!" Brendan cursed.

Penny's tone reflected her frustration at Meri's recounting. "Nothing about this makes sense. "You say Cyn approached you with a proposal. I'm sure there was more to it than just faking your death."

"She'd lost track of Richard, and she wanted my help finding him. She made me a vampire so that I could assist her."

Penny shook her head in disbelief. "Do you think if you say it fast enough, and with enough confidence that no one will catch the flaws in your little story? You know that isn't the way it works, Meri. You were a minister and a missionary. Both Ceese and Richard shared this with me. You wouldn't survive the ordeal of being cursed. Your soul *was* accounted for."

Meri grabbed Penny's right hand, with both of his. With one on her wrist and the other on the back of her hand, Meri placed her palm on his chest and held it there. For the next few seconds, and long enough for a short conversation to have happened, the two stood like that, and then Penny took her hand back.

"Who holds your soul, Meri? If you're not cursed, where is it? Or is Kyle right? Are you just faking not being a vampire to get close to a meal?"

Chapter 9

IT NAVIGATED DOWN FROM its post in the basement's rafters and circled the coffin. It floated over and under, its movements ritualistic and dark, hinting at a malevolent origin and nature. The saturnine celebration continued in the musty darkness until a visible face formed—the face of a seductress, the face of evil. It eyed the coffin wantonly. *All mine,* it hissed, *Finally, all mine.* It entered the coffin and positioned itself to strike the vulnerable neck of the one resting there but drew back at the last second.

What's this? Fresh bite marks?

It recoiled and released a banshee-like shriek that shook dust from rafters; particles that spun into a blizzard upon its rushed exit.

* * *

"What do ye mean, where's his soul?" Brendan asked.

Penny, uncertain of whether the big man could hold up under more bad news, carefully reported her findings. "There's nothing there."

Brendan's eyes wobbled tears. "That can't be. If ye nae be cursed—"

"Please," Meri interrupted, his expression begging for forgiveness, for understanding, for mercy. "This isn't your burden to bear, Bren. Everything I did—it falls on me and me alone. Please tell me you understand that."

"Who are ye? Nae, the man I knew—or thought I knew. After ye were gone, I took yer place. I led the mission. I wanted to be *just* like ye. Now I don't even know who ye are. Whatever ye did, ye shouldn't have done."

"But I did do it, and nothing can change that."

Jaw clenched and tense as a bow pulled tautly, Brendan added, "Richard would nae approve of yer actions either. I can assure ye."

He had that look and Penny knew, based on how Brendan physically fought with Richard on the night he arrived at the castle, tossing Richard around like a rag doll, that his emotions were beyond the scope of what most considered normal and it seemed that he was just as volatile even without Zade's werewolf influence.

"I think," Penny said, her tone level, "that we should all calm down."

"I promise," Meri said, "things aren't as bad as they seem."

The shriek from the basement, now traveling up the stairs, worked to undermine his words.

72

Cyn No More

Penny's face, along with everyone else's, showed shock. "Not as bad as they seem? Indeed, it appears things are much worse."

* * *

A frantic Kyle stumbled around like television's fictional Barney Fife. Arms flailing and eyes bulging, he rushed the door, but it swung shut in his face. He twisted the locked knob, practically sobbing. "What do we do now?"

The disembodied wail rose to a deafening crescendo before falling to silence. Everyone backed away from a thicker-than-mist blackness that crept in and filled the room, suffocatingly thick. The manifestation breathed, pulsed, and spoke, the decidedly feminine voice dripping venom.

"How dare you defy me?" it said to no one in particular.

Meri answered.

"I—I am sorry," he stammered in reply. "But I won't let you have him. I *won't*! He's my son."

"Do I need to remind you that long ago we struck a bargain? Made a deal? You chose to help me if I helped you. You gave your word *and* your soul. I should send it straight to hell for what you've done here. Or maybe," it taunted, "maybe you should suffer a little more first—for your treachery."

Sue Dent

The thick blackness gathered in the center of the room and spun into a cyclonic fury. Its force swept pictures from walls, knocked lamps off tables, and in a final assault, pulled an ornate rod holding thick curtains from the wall. A rush of sunlight filled the room, creating a reverse-blindness. Glass exploded out of the window frame, an opening through which the blackness exited.

Kyle was the first to speak in the lull that followed, unsteadily taking to his feet. "Please tell me it's gone?"

Rodney lowered the forearm he used to shield his eyes and warbled the first line of Manfred Mann's *Blinded by the Light,* mangling the original lyrics on purpose, ". .wrapped up like a douche another bo—" Cassie whipped her head around "—in the night," he quickly finished.

Brendan shuffled through debris while calling out to his missing parent, his heavy boots crunching glass as he went.

"There," Ceese said, pointing, "beneath the wardrobe. I heard something." And indeed, there was a rustling from beneath the large piece of furniture that had toppled over onto the felled drapes. Brendan rushed over and put a shoulder to the dresser but couldn't seem to move it.

Ceese turned to Rodney, an anxious look on her face. Seeing her expression, Rodney rushed to help

74

Cyn No More

Brendan. Together the two managed to set the wardrobe upright.

Brendan went straight to work on the pile of curtains beneath it, reaching down and pulling up, grunting as he tugged. "Aye, he's wrapped up good an' tight."

"Be careful," Penny advised, "there's glass everywhere. You're already bleeding."

Brendan stopped and examined his hand. "Aye, but it nae be my blood." He stared down at his now visible parent. "It be Father's."

Penny leaned over and gasped. "The knife wound is back. And those are fresh bite-marks as well." Brendan shifted to get a better look. A beam of sunlight shot past his shoulder. Meri's eyes flew open. He forced out a keen and agonizing moan. Brendan leaned back in to block the light once more.

"He's a vampire again," Ceese gasped in shock.

Chapter 10

PENNY LOOKED TO BRENDAN. "We need to get him out of here. There's a windowless room across the hall. We can take him there."

Brendan felt around and found Meri's waist through the bulk of the curtains yet struggled to lift him. He adjusted his stance for more leverage and tried again but still couldn't bring Meri's dead weight up to stand.

Penny leaned in to help. Brendan reacted with a stern and frustrated, "I got this."

"You're going to have to let me help you—for Meri's sake. We've got to get him out of here, and the sooner, the better."

Reluctantly, Brendan conceded, and within seconds Meri hung limply between the pair, looking very much like the recently dead. Cassie swooped in to cover the once-again-vampire with one of the curtain panels from the downed rod, protecting him from the sunlight pouring in. Across the room, Kyle pulled and twisted at the locked doorknob, falling back when the door magically *whooshed* open. The surprise of it sent him tripping backward.

Cyn No More

"I heard the commotion from downstairs," Geoffrey said as he took the master key from its lock and entered.

Kyle recovered and bolted past the butler. "It's about time."

Meri's blood-stained shirt caught Geoffrey's eye.

"He's going to need a new bandage," Penny said. "A complete redressing."

Professionally trained to serve without asking questions, Geoffrey nodded and headed off to gather the necessary items.

Out in the hall, Cassie took quick steps and opened the door to the room that Penny referenced a moment ago. She went in, prepped the bed, pulled back covers, and moved extra pillows out of the way.

Brendan and Penny walked in with Meri; Brendan's forehead creased with worry. "He nae looks good," he said, after carefully removing the curtain panel and tossing it in a corner.

Geoffrey returned with bandages and effectively redressed the wound.

"Aye, now it's back to getting him to feed."

Ceese turned toward an apparition that formed from thin air directly in front of Rodney and spoke to it. "You can get him to feed, can't you? I mean, that's why you're here, right?"

"Me?" Rodney said.

Penny sensed the new energy in the room and said to Rodney, "I don't think she's talking to you?"

"She's looking right at me?"

The apparition brought a silencing finger to its lips, suggesting that Ceese keep her presence anonymous. Ceese nodded yet continued to talk. "But you can help him."

"Did Josh say something to you?" Had Josh told Ceese what happened the other night.

The apparition nodded in response to Ceese's question, and again, Rodney thought she was nodding at him. "Alright. I'll try it. Kyle, go get me those two units of blood from the other room."

Kyle pushed off the door frame and hitched a thumb over his shoulder. "*That* room?"

"Yes, *that* room."

"First off, I'm not your servant. And second, *Ha—!* I'm never going into *that* room again."

"Then I guess I'll go myself." Rodney bumped past Kyle on his way out and then again upon returning with the two blood pouches. "G-Man," he said, "think fast." He tossed over one of two blood-pouches then delivered the second one directly to the butler, much like a quarterback executing a handoff.

Cyn No More

He then continued past Geoffrey and over to the discarded curtain panel in the corner. Picking it up, he shook it. Embedded glass shards tinkled loose. He took a sizeable one from the floor and walked around to the opposite side of the bed. "Blood pouch equals 'cold pet,'" he said to the butler.

"Pardon?"

"*Cold pet*," Rodney emphasized.

"Ah, yes," the butler recalled. 'Cold pet' is what Geoffrey called the dead rabbit that Rodney brought him to send to his researcher friends in the states. And while things were less confusing for him, the unwitting observers could only wonder.

Rodney settled on the edge of the bed, pushed his left sleeve up. With the glass shard, he drew a thin line on his wrist—and squeezed until blood ebbed through.

Geoffrey sat across from him at the ready, palming one of the two blood pouches.

Rodney took in a deep breath and eased his now bleeding wrist closer to Meri's mouth and nose, just as he'd done the night Josh had come to him. Closer and closer until all at once, the vampire's cold eyes flew wide-open.

Ceese gasped delight. "It's working!"

Rodney turned his head at her excitement and then suddenly opened his eyes wide. "Biting, biting, he-he's biting—ow, ow, ow . . ."

79

Geoffrey moved in with the pouch of blood, but the vampire ignored him. Geoffrey let the pouch fall to the bed and instead maneuvered around, placed two fingers and a thumb on either side of the vampire's jaws, and attempted to pry its mouth open, but the jaws held a pit-bull-like-grip on Rodney's wrist. Cassie leaned in and took the blood pouch that Geoffrey abandoned and smeared it with blood that dripped down.

"Here," she said, handing it back to the butler, "try it now."

The vampire enthusiastically struck and, once free, Rodney shot up to stand and cradled his bleeding arm, the shock of what he had just done—again—settling in.

Chapter 11

"THANK YOU," RODNEY SAID to Cassie.

Cassie swung around to face him. "I'm sorry, but did you just thank me?"

"Yeah. Thanks for finally doing something helpful. What made you think to do that with the blood pouch anyway?"

Cassie rolled her eyes. "You know. It's how Richard stopped Josh's attack on Kyle back at the apartment—shortly after Henderson cursed Josh. You also know that right after that, you attempted to stop Josh from attacking Kyle by launching *my* potted plant by its macramé rope at Josh's head, for all the good that did."

Rodney smiled at the memory. "Oh yeah. And throwing that plant at Josh's head did a lot of good. I'll never have to worry about that fu—"

"Use that word, and you'll be looking for another place to stay once we get back home."

"I was going to say *funky,* 'Church Lady.'"

"And don't call me that."

"Like I was saying," he continued, "I don't have to worry about that funky fern shedding its dry, dead leaves on me anymore."

Brendan moved up behind Rodney, his hot breath cascading down the back of the punk's neck. He reached around and took hold of Rodney's bleeding wrist. "Aye, and why do I see another set of toothy imprints. What are those marks from?"

Rodney yanked his arm back. "None of your business."

Brendan's eyes narrowed. "Means ye've done this before? That's what ye said to Ceese a wee moment ago."

"So, what if I did?"

"Why'd it take ye so long to try it again? Father could've died."

"What is it with you? I helped him, didn't I? He's feeding, isn't he?"

"Nearly too late," Brendan growled.

"If I were to guess," Cassie said, "I'd say it had something to do with incentive." And she nodded sideways toward Ceese.

"Well, she did ask," Rodney said, defending his actions, "which is more than any of you did."

Cyn No More

In one quick motion, Brendan forced Rodney up against a wall, cupped his large hand around the young man's throat.

"That's some gratitude," Rodney sputtered, futilely tugging at Brendan's wrist until, just like that, it came free. Brendan immediately slammed him back against the wall with his thick forearm.

"Stop," Ceese said, torn between her allegiance to her brother and her feelings for Rodney. "Let him go. You'll hurt him."

Rodney stared into Brendan's angry eyes. He squinted, and just loud enough for Brendan's ears to hear, he said, "if only you were as strong as you used to be. Then you could show me."

Brendan shoved harder, knocking the breath out of Rodney before turning him loose. "I wish I knew what ye see in 'im," he said to Ceese. He gave the group his back and stormed out.

Geoffrey turned to Rodney. "I don't have all that I need to tend to your wrist, but if you follow me to the kitchen, I have a well-stocked first aid kit there."

Once in the hall, the butler turned left. "I thought the kitchen was that way," Rodney said, pointing off to the right.

"It's also this way."

Sue Dent

Rodney followed the butler into a dark room and flipped a switch on the wall, but no light came on. "Can't afford light bulbs?"

Geoffrey continued across the room and opened a door on the opposite wall. Rodney came up behind him, peered over his shoulder. "Oh, look, it's a dark closet to go with the dark room." The butler flipped a switch and a long corridor filled with light.

"Ahh, a dark closet that's bigger on the inside," Rodney marveled.

The butler smiled; an expectant look covered his face. "Indeed. In that regard, the corridors are much like a Tardis."

Rodney scrunched his brows in confusion. "Huh?" The butler's expectant look fell. "I'm sorry. Am I supposed to know what that means? You look so disappointed."

Geoffrey offered a tight smile. "I'll get over it."

The pair moved along.

Rodney gawked at the classically dated architecture all around; stone walls and arched framework. "This place is creepy. Looks haunted."

"I fear it is haunted—by a pair of identically twinned spirits; Missy and Millicent. Quite the tricksters."

"You're putting me on."

Cyn No More

"Except I have proof." The butler pointed to a slightly darker area on his forehead. "When I first arrived, I went about learning how to navigate the servant's corridors. One split into two with no plaque to direct. The two ghosts appeared saying they could help. Each pointed but not at the same passage. Each claimed they were the one I should believe. I made my choice and heard giggling once my head hit the low hanging ceiling."

"So, you're clumsy. Doesn't prove the girls are ghosts."

"I wasn't so far away that I couldn't see them when I looked back. The two disappeared into thin air. One second both girls were there, and the next second— gone like a puff of smoke."

Another turn and Rodney moved on from Geoffrey's ghost story. "It is like a maze in here. How do you keep from getting lost?"

"Well, I've only been at it for a few days, but I'd have to say, trial-and-error—and those." He pointed out directional plaques affixed to the walls as they passed them. "I've memorized a few routes."

They walked down a short set of stairs, then a longer hall, then more steps. "We're almost to the kitchen now." He pointed at a plaque that verified this.

"I'm not sure that this is a quicker way," Rodney said, looking over his shoulder, "but it's certainly a more interesting one." And a route he would not willingly take again. He had enough worries with werewolves and vampires. He didn't need ghosts in his life too.

Chapter 12

GEOFFREY PUSHED THROUGH A door that exited into a large walk-in pantry. Turning to a cabinet, he removed a first aid kit that occupied a middle shelf. He took items from inside of it: gauze, medical tape, antiseptic, and said, "Give me your arm."

The butler doused a cotton ball with alcohol and began to wipe at Rodney's injured wrist. Rodney hissed in air and pulled his arm away.

"That stings!"

The butler frowned and took the arm back. He put gauze over the wound and secured it with the tape. "There, that should do. We'll need to change that later today and clean it again to make sure infection doesn't set in."

"Or rabies," Rodney muttered pathetically.

"Perhaps if you'd been bitten by a werewolf." Geoffrey turned back to the cabinet. "And might I offer you a word of advice. Perhaps it would be in your best interest to try and get along with Master Brendan."

"Why? Apparently, he isn't *werewolf-strong* anymore," he said, drawing air quotes with his fingers.

"Yes, I saw that you were able to break his hold at one point, but then a gentle shove knocked the breath out of you."

Two driving gloves were in a front pocket of Geoffrey's coat. He smoothly removed one and upon turning around, struck Rodney across the cheek with it.

Rodney jerked surprise. "Hey, what was that for?"

"It's how one proposes a challenge. I challenge you to be the young man you are most certainly capable of being."

Rodney laughed easily. "Yeah, well, I am who I am, and I don't plan on changing anytime soon." He turned to leave.

"You haven't heard my challenge," Geoffrey said to his back.

"I've heard enough."

Geoffrey cleared his throat loudly. "There's a little financial matter I need to discuss with you."

"What? Are you going to charge me for dressing a wound? Put it on my tab."

"Your tab has already exceeded the worth of our budding friendship. Presently, you owe me three-hundred pounds or rather five-hundred American dollars for the postage of your 'cold pet.'" Rodney looked glum. "The one you wanted delivered to your researcher friend in the States with expedited shipping.

Cyn No More

And then there's the bit I paid for having Master Kyle flown over first class—"

Rodney put up both hands. "Okay, okay, I get it! I owe you money. But you said I could pay you back as I got it."

"Indeed, but since you've no income presently," the butler said, his tone patient yet firm, "I've decided to help you out. You can do chores around the castle instead."

"You mean I can do chores, and that'll cover what I owe you?"

"If you accept my challenge."

Rodney pointed toward his right cheek. "You mean when you assaulted me with your glove."

"Swatted," Geoffrey said dryly.

A sly smile perched on Rodney's pierced lips. "Ah, blackmail. I didn't know you had it in you. I'm guessing you have chores lined up already?"

Geoffrey opened a lower cabinet door and took out a plunger. "Yes. Take this to the water-closet upstairs and—"

Rodney's eyes grew wide. "Hold up, water closet?"

"The 'gents,' the loo—the 'little boys' room?"

"Um, no—no, thank you. The deals off. I don't do toilets or privies or whatever you call them here."

Sue Dent

"Very well then," Geoffrey said and grabbed up the handset of an archaic rotary house phone that hung on a nearby wall. He pressed it to his ear and proceeded to dial three numbers. "I shall arrange to have you dropped off at the nearest airport." The receiver emitted an odd droning noise as Geoffrey waited to be connected.

"Dude, that isn't even a real phone."

But then Geoffrey started talking, and squawking noises came back in return. "Yes, Vinson, I've someone who needs a ride."

"Who is Vinson?

Geoffrey covered the mouthpiece with a hand. "The chauffeur I hired. You'll need to gather your things together quickly. He doesn't like to be kept waiting. I'm not sure how he got fired from his last job, but it likely had something to do with his lack of patience. Not necessarily a professional attribute, but I was hard-pressed to find someone who wouldn't ask questions." Geoffrey went back to his conversation but barely got a word out before Rodney snatched the handset away and returned it to its hook.

"Okay, I'll do it. Geez, you can't take a joke very well, can you?"

A tight smile held up a corner of his mouth. "Not my strong suit, I suppose."

Cyn No More

"Well, as far as this chore goes, I've been up all night chasing a werewolf through the woods, and I'm really tired."

"Of course," Geoffrey nodded. "It can wait until after you've rested."

"And if I back out of the deal altogether?" Geoffrey reached for the house phone handset once more. "Okay," Rodney said, blocked the butler's arm with one of his, grasped the plunger by its long handle with his other hand. "Just checking."

"I hoped you'd see it my way." Geoffrey exited the pantry into the kitchen.

"My hourly rate is pretty high," Rodney said to his back.

Geoffrey's voice trailed as he walked away. "I set the rate."

Chapter 13

AFTER RODNEY LEFT WITH the butler. Kyle pushed off the door frame. "I'm outtie," he said to the three left in the room with Meri, and he threw a hand sign as though he belonged to some gang; a few fingers bent and some straight.

Meri slept.

"I guess there's no reason for us to stay either," Penny said. "It will be a while before Meri wakes, and goodness knows we could all use some rest ourselves."

Ceese tracked unseen movement with her eyes, turned to Penny. "I'll be going to my room now," she said, cold-shouldered Cassie as she left.

Taking Penny's suggestion about getting some rest to heart, Cassie exited into the hall after Ceese. Looked back over her shoulder when, surprisingly, Penny didn't follow. "Are you coming?"

"What—oh, yes. Of course. Just thought I saw something." With one more quick look, she pulled the door closed behind her.

Conversing as they walked, Cassie said, "I can't believe Richard's a vampire again, especially after all he went through to have his curse lifted. And he doesn't even recall what happened last night, let alone the past week in New York."

"It will all come back to him, dear," Penny said as they moved down the stairs. "You just have to be patient."

"I suppose that would be easier to do if he could at least remember who I am. I mean, he remembers you —and quite affectionately it seems."

"You shouldn't let that bother you. Richard's just drawing from fragments of memories. There's a difference between those feelings and the feelings he undoubtedly has for you. He'll piece it all together soon enough."

Cassie stopped in front of her door and Penny, at hers across the way. "Grandmother," Cassie asked, "how do you do it? How do you just stop loving Richard?"

Penny bit at her lower lip and closed her eyes tightly as she faced her door. "Let's talk about it later. After we've all had some rest."

* * *

Penny waited until she heard the soft thud of Cassie's door close. Afterward, she crossed her room and went inside her dressing closet. Sliding her fingers along the raised edge of a wall panel, she found the catch and released it. An opening behind it led to the servant's corridors. She entered and thought, *I shouldn't be doing this. I shouldn't.* Seeing Richard as a vampire pushed emotions to the surface she couldn't ignore. And being younger once again, or at least younger than the eighty years she was before Ceese restored her youth—well, she just had to make sense of it all, for Cassie's sake and hers. Just days ago, she told Cassie she no longer had romantic feelings for Richard. She needed to be sure this was still true.

She followed the corridor around, took the steps that led down, and exited through a door that opened into the basement. Uncertain of her decision, she hesitated and then reasoned. *I've come this far. I might as well check on him and make sure he's all right.*

She eased the coffin's hinged lid open, looked down at the vampire inside, and all at once felt faint. *No! Not a vision. Not now.* Nevertheless, the basement walls melted away, and the musty air became a briny ocean breeze. Instead of staring down into the coffin, she now stared over the edge of a very tall cliff and at the moonlit crests of waves below; waves that gleamed white in the darkness and broke against the rocky, jagged peaks of rugged coastline. She became an active participant in a vision, a memory, as real as when it happened so many years ago.

Hearing someone coming, she grabbed up the length of her ankle-long dress and rushed to hide, ducked behind a sizeable rock formation. Peeking, she saw a fashionably attired young man, his back to her as he stepped to the very edge of the cliff. He raised both arms from his side.

"Don't!" she shouted, darted out to try and stop him.

Startled, he rocked back on his heels, swung his arms for balance, and spun around to glare at her, his longer unbound hair, caught up in the stiff breeze, whipping about like angry Medusa snakes. "What the devil is wrong with you? You very nearly had me plunging to my death!"

"Excuse me? I stopped you from jumping."

"I nearly fell from fright."

She studied him for a long moment, decided to play along. "I'm sorry if I misinterpreted your actions. It wasn't my intention."

The words sounded sincere, yet he seemed unconvinced. "Forgive me if I don't believe you?"

"Forgive? There's some irony. Forgiveness isn't something that comes easily to our kind, now is it."

"*Our* kind?" he said with an air of suspicion. "Whatever do you mean?"

"Oh, you're new at this, aren't you? Though I will admit, I didn't sense it right away either." She stared sideways at the ascot he wore. "What are you hiding there?"

She reached out toward it.

Sue Dent

He swatted her hand away. "I'm fairly certain I'm not hiding anything."

"Then why not let me take a peek?"

She reached out again.

He swatted again. Over-swatted and lost his footing altogether.

Over the edge, he went.

"Oh, dear!" she said as his arms and legs flailed about wildly. She searched the ground for a sizeable boulder, one that would bring her closer to his weight. Seeing one, she took it up, cradled it in the crook of her left arm, and jumped after him. Coming up beside him, she shouted over the rush of wind. "Give me your hand."

He tried, but they couldn't connect. Finally, she managed to snag one before it flew past her. The boulder no longer needed; she let it drop. At the ground rushing mercilessly toward them, she worked to stop their fall. With what energy she had left, she brought them to a jerking halt inches away from the jagged peaks of coral where they dangled like two marionettes suspended by magical strands of invisible rope.

Chapter 14

THE HIGH SALINE CONTENT of ocean water worked to drain her of the energy she needed to get them to shore. She moved at once to take advantage of what remained, moved both into a vertical and upright position. A wave crashed nearby; a cloud of sea spray overtook them. Down they went, splashing into the shallows.

Knee-deep and then ankle-deep, they waded onshore. She came out of her soaked dress and advised her new friend to do likewise. "If you want any relief from the itching and burning, that is."

Modestly dressed in her undergarments, she went about collecting seaweed and driftwood, constructed a crude and rudimentary clothesline, coaxed a fire to life, and draped her things over it to dry. She relocated a larger piece of driftwood and sat.

He walked over to drape his clothes as well. She stifled an unbidden laugh.

"I'm sorry. Did I do a funny thing without knowing it?"

"No," she said apologetically, "and I realize I must look quite absurd myself, dressed only in my knickers—but you in yours—and still wearing that ascot. Do you ever take it off?"

"No." He sat next to her, fixated on spiraling hot embers that shot off into the night before fizzling out.

She inhaled deeply. "Beautiful, isn't it? The sound of the crashing waves, the smell of the ocean."

"'Scent' of the ocean," he clarified. "And as much as I detest the scent of the ocean, I'd welcome any not overpowered by the scent of—" All at once, he grew silent, put his nose to the air around. A smile broke out across his face. "Indeed, it is as putrid as I recall."

"And that makes you smile?"

"You have no idea."

They passed the next few moments in silence, and then he asked: "How did you know what I was?"

"You mean, how did I know that you were a vampire?"

"Yes."

"After a while, you can tell."

"How did you learn to levitate? Can I do this also?"

"I just sort of figured it out one day while falling to my supposed death. And yes, you can do it as well."

"Will you show me how? I mean, can you teach me?"

"Will you let me look under that ascot?"

Cyn No More

"Why? You already know what's there."

"Yes. So why won't you take it off and let me have a look?"

He turned away from her. "Shame, I suppose."

"Why? It wasn't your fault you were cursed any more than it was mine. Besides, it takes longer for the bite marks to become less distinguishable when you keep them covered like that."

He turned back towards her. "You mean they go away?"

"No," she said gently. "They're just not as noticeable—after a while. See." She leaned in close and pulled her long hair to the side.

"Yes." His eyes followed the line of her jaw, the curve of her neck. She let her hair fall back and turned. His lips were close to hers. And then, they were on hers until — "Ow, ow!"

Both pulled away, used fingers to rub the pain from their throbbing temples.

"There it is," she sighed.

"There what is?"

"Emotion. Strong emotion toward anything other than cursing another is not tolerated."

A short moment later, he fumbled with the knot that held the ascot in place. "There," he said. "You wanted to see."

Sue Dent

She openly gasped. "Two sets of bite marks. That must've been a horrible experience."

"I don't want to talk about it."

"Is that what drove you to the cliff's edge? Shame? Not wanting to go on?"

"No," he said, rather unconvincingly.

"Then, why did you come?"

"Why did you?" he asked in return.

She pulled a book out of a waterproofed pouch. "I come here often to write down my—um—thoughts."

"Are you going to write about what happened this evening?"

"Perhaps," she said, pulled out a pen and ink from the same pouch, prepared it for use. "What should I put?"

"I don't care what you put."

"Well, it's a diary. I like to be accurate. I suppose I'll write down that—well, that I rescued someone tonight."

"Rescued?" he spat out. "You may as well have pushed me."

"I thought you didn't care what I wrote."

"I don't, but what good is a diary if it's filled with lies and inaccuracies? You're the reason I slipped and fell. That's what you should write."

Cyn No More

"And I'm the reason you won't be spending months or longer recovering. Do you have any idea how long it takes to heal from the kind of injuries you would've sustained had you smashed into that coral?"

"Yes, actually. I do. I was hit by a train once."

She drew back in shock. "We certainly are accident-prone. How many other ways have you tried to kill yourself?"

He grew silent and then changed the subject. "Do you suppose you can teach me how to levitate now?"

She shrugged. "I suppose I could, but—um," she gave him a sideways glance, "you have to promise me something first."

"And what would that be?"

"You have to promise me that at some point in the distant future—in the far, far distant future—you must promise to tell me why you came here tonight."

"Pfft, why not. If we're still together and you even remember."

"We'll be together," she said with some confidence. "And I'll definitely remember. After all, I'm writing it in my diary, aren't I?"

* * *

All at once, the basement walls closed back in, and Penny pushed up from the basement floor. She looked in on Richard one last time and traced his jawline with the back of her hand. He wouldn't be aware for some time, so she didn't worry that he might wake and find her standing over him. "I will always love you, Richard Bastóne. Always." She then lowered the coffin's lid and left the way she came.

* * *

Hearing Grandmother's voice, Cassie stopped midway down the basement steps. "I will always love you, Richard Bastóne," came the words she didn't expect to hear. Or did she? *Of course, you still love him. How could you not?* Cassie turned to head back to her room, tears streaming. *Why did I even come down to check on Richard? I could've gone to bed without having my fears confirmed, that Grandmother still loves him.*

Chapter 15

BRENDAN PACED THE WELL-MANICURED castle grounds, Rodney's punk-voice echoing in his head with an ease that was both irritating and unwelcome. "You're not as strong as you used to be," the voice repeated over and over.

Brendan grew angrier with each stomping step. Rodney's words held a truth he couldn't deny; an unsettling reminder that he was once again mortal.

Completely mortal.

"Eegit," the big man seethed, turning sharply on a heel and pacing the other way. A half-buried stump at the forest's edge caught his attention. In need of release, he charged it and kicked. But the stump did not fly into the air as hoped. Instead, it stayed rooted, his foot hitting it with a bone-cracking *thud*.

Nevermore aware of his shortcomings, the once-upon-a-time warrior, hobbled, shoulders stooped and head hanging to his room. Once there, he took off his duster, his shirt, and removed one boot. The other boot he left alone, not wanting to deal with the throbbing foot inside. Laying back on his bed, he let his head drop to his pillow and waited. For the past few evenings and after Penny helped him with his grief over his beloved's death years ago, she came to him. His Gwen. Tonight, however, all he felt was a familiar heaviness, as raw as a wound with its scab ripped off. Torturous, heavy sobs shook his big frame until, at last, he slept.

* * *

The unseen visitor in Meri's room placed an airy palm on the vampire's forehead and induced a particular nocturnal imagining into his otherwise dreamless sleep.

Along the banks of the River Forth, the river of his childhood, Meri spied a large number of the *doine maithe*. The seventh son of a seventh son, Meri understood not to engage them, recalling Father's words that it was always best to let them be or to let them make the first move. But Meri felt compelled and drew closer. The knot of gentry untangled upon his approach and allowed him to walk amongst them. He followed their gloomy stares to the water's edge. A young woman's body floated face down, her hair ebbing and flowing with the current, trapped air causing her dress to bob out around her. Thinking the gentry brought him here to rescue the girl, he scrambled down the embankment and leaped into freezing, cold water that took his breath but not his resolve. Reaching her after only a few strokes, he turned her over, swam with her back to the shore, dragged her to flat ground, and pushed her wet hair from her face.

Cyn No More

It was Julia from the orphanage. The young woman he was courting. The one he had been waiting to tell Father about.

Now frantic, he positioned his hands over her chest and pressed rhythmically. Up, down, up, down until his arms burned from fatigue. He continued until he gave in to exhaustion. Settled back on his heels, he took note of the complacent expressions on the faces of the fey all around.

"You brought me here to save her. She's one of you, isn't she? She's part of your clan."

A tall-hatted, bearded fey spoke up. "She is."

"So, bring her back. I pulled her out of the water. Do something."

"We need your help. We need a promise."

"Yes, of course. Whatever it is, I'll swear to it. Whatever you want from me, I'll give."

"She did not fall in the river by her own hand," the tall-hatted fey with the beard said, "and the one responsible will try again. We need you to promise to protect her. She is no longer safe with us."

"Yes, yes," he said nodding. "I swear to it. I promise. Just bring her back. Bring Julia back."

He turned at the coughing gasps behind him, and the dream ended.

* * *

Sue Dent

It took the crew four hours to finish the repairs to the upstairs bedroom. Geoffrey, satisfied with their work, led the five men downstairs with the promise of extra pay for work done quickly and quietly.

On their way out, Geoffrey escorted them through a hall that rumbled with snores; snores that grew louder the further down the hall they walked.

The sheer volume got the best of one cockney-accented worker. "Wha' do you 'ave 'oled up in 'here, a Grizzly?"

The outburst brought stunned silence from his peers who held their collective breath at the caustic look on the butler's face when the snores abruptly stopped. If the owner of the snores woke up, it might cost them their bonus. A few quick snorts later, the loud rattling started up again. Looking less tense, Geoffrey continued to lead the men down the hall.

Standing next to the company van, one concerned worker asked the butler, "What Archie said back there, you won't be holding that again' us, right? I mean, we done the work nice and quiet jus' like you asked."

"I suppose not," the butler replied. "But I do need to know that each of you will keep quiet about anything you saw here today—anything that might be worth talking about. Anything out of the ordinary. Not a word to anyone."

Cyn No More

The men took turns looking at each other. "Out of the ordinary?" one man questioned in return. "You mean like them two coffins in the basement?"

"Or all the blood what I cleaned up in that bedroom," another surmised.

"Or the other coffin in the outbuilding," another added.

"*Or*," Archie emphasized, "that grizzly what's hibernatin' in that room."

"Precisely," Geoffrey replied. "Or anything else for that matter." The butler pressed several bills into each worker's palm. "So, we have an understanding then?"

One worker looked down at the money in his hand and frowned slightly. "Where's the rest of it—the rest of what you promised?"

"You'll receive your bonus via post and after two weeks. An incentive to keep quiet about what you've seen today should you be inclined to talk about it."

All seemed to accept the reasoning. And why wouldn't they? He had already paid them more than they usually received for a job well done.

Chapter 16

CLAYTON HENDERSON WOKE UP thirsting for blood and with at least a hundred thumb-sized vampire bats suckling on his flesh, the amplified lure of a vampire in desperate need drawing them in like flies to a corpse.

He grabbed up his tweed-jacket pillow and began swatting at the pesky varmints as he rushed to flee his cave-refuge in search of a meal to stop the lure.

* * *

Philip Darden, head of Financial Affairs at Templeton University, saw his cousin's name flash across his vibrating cell phone's screen. "Son of a —" Angrily, he snatched the device up. "Where the hell have you been?"

"Cousin, you sound agitated."

"How should I sound? My director of Bio-Engineering, who I highly recommended for the job, has disappeared without a word to anyone."

"I apologize—"

"Apologize?" Philip spat out. "Do you have any idea how difficult it was to convince the board to hire you in the first place? Your jaded background in stem cell research certainly didn't help."

"I signed the confidentiality agreement, didn't I? And at least I'm out of your house. Wasn't that the main objective?"

"That's beside the point," Philip muttered. "As it stands, the board is about to meet on your behalf, and I have to tell them something. Do you have any suggestions?"

"Tell them there's been a death in the family, and I need some time off."

"Wouldn't I know about a death in the family? I can't tell them that."

"Fine, then I'll send a friend of mine over to fill in until I return. He's more qualified than I am to teach my classes. His name is Lucien Savine. I'll get him to call you."

A dumbfounded Philip replied, "You can't just send someone in to take your place."

"I think the board will see it my way. I'm fairly certain they don't want to risk losing their precious 4.7-million-dollar grant because they don't have anyone to teach my classes. As I said, Lucien is more than qualified, and I'll return to my duties—uh—*soonish?*" Henderson ended the call even as Philip continued to rant.

* * *

Sue Dent

The land-line phone in Henderson's basement lab, a room comprised of discarded equipment from Henderson University's renovated-with-grant-money facility, rang. Lucien looked up from a microscope to check the caller ID and quickly picked up the receiver. He answered the phone in Russian but continued in heavily accented English. "You have our werewolf, no?"

Henderson sighed. "Not exactly. I'm still working on it. How are things going on your end?"

Lucien held the phones cordless receiver in one hand and walked back to the microscope he abandoned to answer the call. He peered through the eyepiece at the slide on its stage. "I am seeing much hope for our plans. The stem cell samples are multiplying nicely to being infused."

"And the chance of coaxing them into gametes?"

Lucien straightened. "That too is coming along. I have already begun preparations. But you sound less optimistic than I."

Henderson did a quick rehash of all that had gone wrong. "Bottom line, our ex-werewolf is still just that—an ex-werewolf."

"Why not use infected stem cells, same as you did to become vampire to turn her yourself?"

Cyn No More

"Don't think I haven't thought about that. But I don't have enough workable werewolf stem cells or a delivery system."

"You may have enough now," Lucien said, staring back down at the microscope's slide. "And a darted tranquilizer gun loaded with werewolf stem cells would work as a delivery system. No?"

At one point in his career, Lucien worked closely with rogue elements within the Russian military to weaponize biochemical compounds. Henderson knew this and beamed like a proud parent at his partner's possible solution to their dilemma.

"That's brilliant," he said. "Absolutely brilliant." And then, almost as an afterthought, he said, "there's a cell phone in my top desk drawer. Charge it. I'll be calling and texting you on that from now."

Chapter 17

IF RICHARD'S YOUNG MAID Marissa had been chewing gum the day she witnessed the menacing werewolf carrying an unconscious, and elderly, Madam Penelope across the castle lawn, she would've swallowed it on the spot. As it were, she allowed a growling and snarling Ceese to use her as her mouthpiece: "She won't hurt her," she told her employer. "She would never hurt her. Penny is her friend."

Marissa lived all of her nineteen years at the castle, the only child of her servant parents. She now carried on in her parent's stead. Her life was ordered and structured and predictable, just the way she thought she liked things. But as time passed, she learned that she no longer knew what she liked. Moreover, she didn't understand the way she felt whenever the large man with one arm came around. Even now, when he entered the kitchen, her stomach flip-flopped and felt altogether out of sorts. Her face flushed red and grew notably warmer.

Seeing him move toward the refrigerator, she abandoned salad preparation for the evening meal to assist him; grabbed a clean plate from a cupboard, offered to fill it with leftovers from the refrigerator.

Cyn No More

"If ye could," he said in reply.

Marissa took the microwaved food over to the small round dinette table and set the plate in front of him.

"Thank ye," he said before digging in.

Half-way through his meal, Geoffrey entered from the hall.

"I trust you slept well," the butler said. "I saw you a few moments ago and noticed you favoring one leg."

"Cramp," Brendan answered around a mouthful of chicken, adding to the lie after swallowing, "charley horse."

Penny wandered in next, poured herself a cup of tea. "Mind if I join you?" she asked innocently.

Brendan's eyes narrowed. "It be yere castle," he said with an air of contempt. "Sit where ye like."

Penny took the chair across from him, stirred at her tea to cool it. "Still in a foul mood, I see," she said, recalling his encounter with Rodney earlier that morning.

Brendan speared her with sharp words, "I've a right to be in a foul mood, *seer*. Thanks to ye."

* * *

Cassie awoke to the words, 'someone's coming.' She pushed up onto her elbows, looked around. Twilight darkened the room, but a small lamp offered enough light for her to see that no one was there.

Sue Dent

The last time she heard voices was in the emergency room. 'Bring them home,' is what she heard. Grandmother referred to these manifestations as visions. But for her, at least so far, there were no images. She listened for more words. Not hearing any, she dropped back down to her bed and closed her eyes.

A minute later, she did hear another voice, and it had her scrambling to her feet, yanking her robe from a nearby chair, shoving her arms into its sleeves, and pulling the sash tight.

"Richard, W-what are you doing here? And how?" She looked at both doors, their locks still set.

"You're not glad to see me?"

"Of course, but—," she struggled with what to say. She reached up and pushed a strand of auburn hair behind an ear.

"Nervous?"

"What—no, why would you ask—" she stopped the question before she finished it, put her hand back down. "You remember me now? You didn't even know who I was this morning." It was the way he looked at her, his tone. She fumbled around her neck for her cross necklace but, it wasn't there.

"How could I ever forget you, Cassie?"

He drew closer, she backed away, bumped the pedestal-nightstand. In horror, she watched her missing cross necklace slide off the other side.

Cyn No More
***

Brendan spoke to her stunned expression. "Like ye nae know what ye did."

"I don't know, Brendan. Suppose you tell me."

He looked away then turned back. "I can nae sense Gwen the way I did after you came to me. She's gone again. Gwen's gone. Whatever ye did—it nac lasted, and the pain of losing her be worse than before."

"What I did was to ease your burden for not being there when Gwen passed, that's all. Are you suggesting something more happened?" The pain in his eyes answered her question. Penny's face showed her frustration at having failed him. "I'm sorry, Brendan. I'm so very sorry. Maybe I can try again—"

"Have ye nae done enough?" he belted out. And then quieter, "Just leave it be."

A terrified scream from down the hall brought the conversation to an end.

Penny shot up from her chair and gasped. "That's Cassie."

Chapter 18

BRENDAN SHOVED AT THE DOOR with a shoulder. Penny gasped at what she saw when it flew opened; Cassie held hostage by Richard, the sharp points of the vampire's fangs parked on her neck.

Without giving it any thought, Brendan charged his vampire brother, wrapped his thick arm around his neck, and managed to free Cassie. Without his werewolf prowess, however, Brendan was as vulnerable as any mortal, and the vampire quickly turned the tables.

Penny watched in fear as Richard pounded Brendan's mid-section until he folded like a ragdoll.

* * *

Josh stepped out of his coffin and removed the elastic band that kept his long, Marley-like dreads in place as he slept and wrapped it around his wrist. He pulled his shirt on and then the bomber jacket he wore like a second skin.

"Ah, you're awake," Meri said. Josh's face lit up. He turned toward his unlikely mentor and bounded over with the exuberance of a dog, happy to see its owner.

Meri motioned for him to tone down his enthusiasm. He put up his hands to guard his chest. "Knife wound," he explained.

Josh reined in his greeting. "Dude, I was worried about you."

"I knew you would be," Meri said, smiled warmly. "That's why I came to see you before going out."

Josh studied the new bandage. "That hasn't healed yet? You fed this morning, didn't you?"

"Yes . . . about that," he said with a decidedly gloomy expression. "There's something I need to tell you. Something you'll hear sooner or later."

Meri told Josh everything that transpired after he left for his coffin earlier that morning and after Josh had delivered him back to his bed with the knife wound.

At the end of the tale, he said, "so, you see, I made Richard a vampire again. I know it doesn't make sense, but I just wanted you to hear it from me so that you understood, so you wouldn't think that I'd given in to my blood lust. As I've told you before; things are very different for me as a vampire. Particularly in this instance with Richard. When I can explain more, I will. For now, though—I can assure you, my soul is still safe and that cursing another is wrong."

Josh shrugged. "Sure, dude."

Meri's eyebrows arched, and he laughed outright. "Really? That's it? No questions? No doubts? You simply believe me?"

"Yeah. Why wouldn't I?"

Meri clasped Josh's shoulder and smiled. "I don't know what I've done to earn your friendship or your trust, but I'm indeed glad to have it."

Afterward, both exited the basement, each heading their separate ways to feed. Josh followed a path around to the front of the castle and stopped at the edge of the woods, jerking his head around when he heard someone scream.

* * *

All eyes were on Josh when he crashed through Cassie's balcony door, even the vampire stopped to look, a one-handed grip on Brendan's shirt collar, his other arm poised to hit him again.

"What are you doing?" Josh said, "That's your brother. Turn him loose."

"As you wish." The vampire lifted Brendan up and with some force, threw the big man across the room. Brendan hit the wall hard, his head meeting it with a

118

sickening thud. His eyes rolled back as he slid unconscious to the floor. "There. I've done what you asked. So, if you'll step aside, I'll be on my way."

Josh, innately aware of the dangers associated with two cursed beings battling and the deadly consequences for both, stepped aside.

With the vampire gone, Penny rushed to Brendan's side. Searched for a pulse and sighed relief. "Josh, could you carry him to his room."

"Yeah, sure," and he carefully scooped Brendan up and stood. With Brendan draped across his arms, he asked. "What just happened here?"

"Can I explain it to you later? Penny said, already comforting a very shaken Cassie.

"Whatever. But you don't have to explain about Richard being a vampire again. I already know what happened."

How could he know? Josh had been in his coffin all morning. He shouldn't know anything about what happened to Richard.

"Meri told me," Josh said before Penny could ask. "He also told me that none of you believed him."

"And you do?"

"Why not? He hasn't lied to me yet?"

"Richard just tried to curse Cassie, and he very likely would've killed Brendan if you hadn't shown up. That's on Meri."

Josh shrugged. "I just know what he told me."

Penny watched the young man's back as he left with Brendan. Had Meri told Josh the same story he told them or was Josh simply that trusting of his new-found friend?

Chapter 19

DR. LAWRENCE LAGUARD LOOKED older than Penny recalled; his salt and pepper hair now solid grey, his wrinkles deeper.

"His room is just down the hall," Penny said, walking with him.

"So, you're Penelope's daughter." His voice rattled with age. "I don't recall her ever mentioning having a child or ever being married for that matter. But Penelope always did play things close to the vest. No denying the resemblance, though. You look just like her."

"I get that a lot," Penny lied, turned the corner.

"How did you know to call me?"

"Your number is by the phone," she said with a smile as she opened a door. "Here's your patient."

With the practiced expertise of a seasoned health care professional, the doctor went right to work. He poked and prodded around Brendan's abdomen, scoped out his eyes, and announced, "he has a slight concussion and a very bruised abdomen. Other than that, he seems fine."

Sue Dent

Geoffrey entered the room on the tail end of the doctor's findings, and Penny was immediately glad she filled the butler in on her little charade; pretending to be her own daughter. "If I may interject," Geoffrey said. "I noticed him limping earlier, favoring his left leg. When I inquired, he told me it was a Charley Horse."

Lawrence moved to have a look, but the boot was stuck-tight. He removed the shoelace, and with Geoffrey's help, managed to prod the shoe off.

"This ankle is broken," Lawrence said after only a cursory examination. "I've got something in my car to set it with." He left and returned with the items he needed; splints, tape. In no time, he had the ankle taken care of set. "I suggest keeping it iced down as well. At least until the swelling is gone."

Geoffrey left to get a cold pack from the kitchen.

Lawrence looked down at the big man. "You know, for all his injuries, he's quite fortunate."

"How do you mean?"

"Well, whoever did this to him did a very good job of not breaking any of his ribs or injuring any vital organs. It's almost as if they didn't intend to hurt him all that seriously."

"I told you, he fell from a ladder."

"These injuries aren't consistent with a fall," he said, looked over his perched-on-the-end-of-his-nose glasses. "Make a fist." She did. "See how the bruises are precisely the shape of your hand, just larger."

"I suppose he could've been involved in a scuffle beforehand," she conceded. "I've no idea where he was before he climbed on that ladder and fell."

She caught Lawrence squinting at her. "I'm sorry," he said. "I can't seem to get over how much you resemble your mother. How is she doing anyway?"

Penny chose her words carefully. How could she explain that a werewolf gave her over forty years of her youth back? On top of that, she wasn't comfortable lying to him. Lawrence had treated her cancer for years until it had gone into remission. He was a good man and a good friend. "She's quite fine and on holiday at the moment. I told her I'd look after things while she was gone."

His voice rose in concern. "She went off on her own?"

"Heavens no," Penny rushed, "not at her age. She's—traveling with a cousin and her husband. The cousin's a—a nurse as well. She's going to stay with them for a while, too, once they return."

All the lying was getting tricky and uncomfortable, and Penny wasn't sure how much longer she could make any of it sound believable. "Can I show you out? I'm sure you'd much rather be at home, especially at this hour."

"It isn't that late," he said, closing up his medical bag. "And it has been nice meeting you in spite of the circumstances." He stood. "If he's hard to keep down," Lawrence said of Brendan, "find someone to sit with him. It wouldn't do him any good to get up on that ankle."

"Oh, I'm sure there's someone we can find for that task." She spoke to the empty doorway. "Marissa, dear, you can come in now." The timid maid, pressed against the wall just outside, entered. Hands folded in front of her. Head down in servitude

"I was just cleaning in the hall, ma'am." But she held nothing to suggest any such activity.

"Perhaps you could put your cleaning on hold to keep an eye on Master Brendan. He's your charge now."

Penny walked Lawrence to the front door. She offered her hand. "Thank you so much for coming by."

He gave her hand a gentle shake. "Glad I could help." Before releasing it, however, he turned it over. "How long has that been there?" Penny tried to keep her gaze neutral. "You need to have that looked at."

"Of course, I'll make an appointment soon. I promise."

She closed the door behind him and caught a breath. Those were the exact words she used so many years

Cyn No More

ago when he first noticed her cancer. But how could it be back?

Chapter 20

VAMPIRES DIDN'T NEED TO breathe to survive, but they needed to breathe to appear normal and not draw unwanted attention. Therefore, as soon as Richard dropped down from levitating, he inhaled to start the process. Briny air blowing in off the Thames filled his lungs. He sputtered, spat and coughed at the assault and decided not to emulate breathing again until he was further away from the river's brackish waters.

He climbed a set of concrete steps up to street-level. A pub across the way caught his attention; neon-lit letters on its window spelling out 'free wi-fi' meant he could call Geoffrey from there.

He made his way through the revelers at the front of the pub, found a table near the back, and pulled out his cell. A busty barmaid in a skimpy sailor uniform arrived before he could place his call.

"You look thirsty. What's your poison?" Her Scottish accent was as detectable as her desire to help him.

He slipped his cell back in a pocket. "My poison," he echoed. "You wouldn't believe me if I told you."

Cyn No More

He spied her nametag. "Is there somewhere we can be alone—Michelle?"

Controlled by the lure, Michelle reached down and took his hand; led him out into the alley, past the dumpster, and around a blind corner.

"How's this?"

"Perfect." He moved around behind her and let the transformation to vampire begin.

Cooperating fully, Michelle tucked a longer ringlet of hair behind an ear and out of the way. The action brought the transformation to an abrupt halt.

"Cassie?" Richard said, momentarily stunned.

At the distraction, the lure grew weak. "My name's not Cassie," Michelle said, shoved a foot between his legs, hooked an ankle and yanked forward. Richard fell hard, and Michelle took advantage; ran without hesitation back to the safety of the bar.

* * *

With an urgency that epitomized his concern, Geoffrey headed to his apartment behind the castle, where he could read the text sent to him by his employer in private. As directed, he gathered cash from a wall-safe, made a few quick phone calls and internet searches, and headed out.

Approximately forty-five minutes later, Geoffrey parked across the street from several pubs, shouldered a satchel from the seat next to him, and crossed over to *The Seafarer*. A small constabulary force mulled around the front of the pub. Geoffrey overheard one officer say that he needed a group to search the alley.

"Excuse me," Geoffrey said. "I couldn't help but overhear, but if you're searching for the man who attacked Michelle, I just saw him."

"What's that? *You* saw him?"

"Yes. Blonde hair, a little longer than shoulder length. He practically walked in front of you just now."

"How is it you know anything about the matter? We've been very tight-lipped."

"Michelle is my niece," he confidently lied. "She called me right after and told me everything, including a description of the suspect. I suggest you hurry if you want to catch him, though."

The officer gave orders that redirected his ragtag group of constables away from the pub. Geoffrey ducked inside. After all, an uncle would want to know how his niece was fairing after such an ordeal.

Michelle stood behind the bar serving drinks. Geoffrey sidled up and took a seat on a stool at the far end.

After she helped the few patrons ahead of him, she made her way down to where he was. "What can I get for you?"

Cyn No More

Geoffrey laid two fifty-pound notes on the bar. "I need you to forget what happened to you in the alley."

She looked at the notes, looked back at him. "What do you mean? Forget the attack? Like bloody hell," she said fiercely.

He laid down another fifty-pound note. "Perhaps you might reconsider."

She inclined her head to study his face. "What? Is he your mate? Is that it?"

Geoffrey replied as decorously as possible. "I'm a gentleman's gentleman. He's my employer and also a friend."

"Yeah. Well, your *friend* has a nasty little habit of dragging women into alleys and assaulting them. If you plan on paying me off," she said, nodding at the notes on the counter, "you're going to have to do better than that."

"I'm prepared to offer more." He took out his cell phone and moved a finger over the screen. He rattled off her address, physical and email, and said, "I see you're two months behind on the rent for your flat."

"How do you know that?"

She tried to peek at the screen. He blocked her view with a hand. "Social Media. You really should be more careful about what you share."

"You've been stalking me? I think that's illegal and bold considering the police are right outside."

"They aren't right outside anymore. And for the record, it isn't illegal to look at someone's public information."

She scooped up the notes he had laid out. "You fancy him, eh, your friend? Why else would you go through all this trouble on his behalf."

"He's a good man."

"Are you not hearing me? I said you fancy him. There's a difference between being a good man and being a good—well, you know. Good men don't drag women into dark alleys against their will."

"I'm not here to defend his actions or to debate yours." He continued to work the phone's screen with his fingers. "Especially since there are witnesses that say you went willingly, practically guiding my employer out. I believe it's on video as well," and he pointed to one of several cameras. She opened her mouth to respond, but he spoke before she could. "You should check your e-mail now."

The cell in her pocket dinged. Her face blanched white. "This is a receipt for the last two past-due payments on my flat. "How did you—"

"I have friends. One acquaintance works for your landlord. I wired him the amount due, and he took care of the rest. So—do we have an accord because I can request that the funds be sent, straight away, back to my account—?" He perched a finger over his phone in wait of her answer.

"No, no," she rushed. "It's good. It's all good. I'm good."

"And you'll clear up the matter with the police—about what really happened?"

"Yes. Definitely. And, uh, if you ever need me to forget anything else—well clearly, you know where to find me. And please do."

Geoffrey nodded and stood. "One other thing. Can you point me toward the exit that leads into the alley?"

"Back of the pub. There's a short hallway. First door on the right."

Geoffrey followed her directions, stepped outside, and walked to the dumpster. He took the turn, prepared to pace off five steps as directed by his employer, but stopped when he felt the practiced, hot breath of the vampire on his neck and heard the words, "that's far enough."

Chapter 21

DINNER WAS LIGHT TO accommodate the small number of diners; Cassie and Penny. Both picked at the food on their plates, eating just enough and declining afters. With all that had happened, neither was in the mood for dessert. Too early for bed but too late for much of anything else, the pair headed to the parlor.

Cassie stood in front of the large window, looking out. After a long moment, she said, "You can have him. You can have Richard."

Penny looked up from sorting through mail on Richard's desk. *What an odd thing to say.* "I beg your pardon?"

Cassie turned from the window. "I heard what you said in the basement this morning—when I went to check on Richard myself."

"Oh? And just what did you hear?"

"I heard you say that you would always love him. And the way you looked at him—" Cassie paused as she struggled with emotion, "you can have him."

"First of all," Penny said gently, walked over to her granddaughter. "I'm quite certain that Richard can make up his own mind about who he wants to be with. And yes, as I've told you before, I will always love him, just not in the way he clearly loves you. So why this long look now?"

"After what he did tonight, nearly cursing me, hurting Brendan—I don't know how I can love him back. It was terrifying."

"You just have to remind yourself that that wasn't Richard."

"Has he ever tried to curse you before?"

"The entire time I've known Richard, he's been a vampire, dear. Of course, he's tried. We lived together for nearly a century. I was a vampire most of that time as well, though. But when I wasn't — yes, he tried. And yes, it can be very frightening. I just always keep a cross around my neck."

She noticed Cassie's cross necklace missing. "Where's yours? You should never take it off."

Cassie felt around her neck. "I didn't, but when I reached for it, when Richard transformed, it wasn't there. I saw it slide off the nightstand when I bumped it trying to get away."

"So, you didn't take it off?"

"No."

Penny shook her head. "I don't like the sound of that."

"How did he get in your room? When Brendan and I got there, all entryways were locked."

"I don't know. I was asleep. I woke up to the words, 'someone's coming' and then I closed my eyes to rest a little longer. That's when I heard Richard say my name."

"You had a vision?"

"More like an auditory vision, but yes. Do you think it was meant to warn me of Richard?"

"Doubtful. You would've heard the voice sooner, in time to react. No. The words you heard must be referencing someone different. Can you recall anything else about it? A feeling? An image?"

Cassie stared as if in deep thought, and then her expression changed to utter dread. "A werewolf. A werewolf is coming."

* * *

Geoffrey froze but not from fear. The lure controlled him. He was aware of his body but not able to react. The vampire pressed against him from behind. Tilted its head in search. Its mouth cruised down the curve of the butler's neck toward the desired spot, dragging the points of its fangs along.

Then it found the silver cross, solemnly blessed by the Pope himself, hanging around Geoffrey's neck. The vampire shoved Geoffrey forward and fell back in agony. The butler rushed to find his bearings, pulled the two blood pouches Richard requested out of the satchel, and set them down. Quick steps took him out of the alley.

Chapter 22

RICHARD SLID INTO THE front passenger seat of the idling car. Dark eyes stared ahead at the park, the Thames behind it mirroring the lights from the streetlamps.

"What's happening to me, Geoffrey? I don't even know how I ended up here." He turned toward the butler, fixated on the blood on his neck, the deep drag marks left by the vampire's fangs—his fangs. He pulled a handkerchief from a pocket, leaned over, wiped, and then held the cloth against the wound.

"Master Richard," Geoffrey said, gently taking hold of the hand against his neck and pulling it away. "I'm fairly certain I won't bleed out before we get back to the castle. I assure you it's — " His words caught in his throat. "Your trembling," he said of the hand he held. "And you look as though you've seen a ghost."

Gripped by sudden terror, Richard stammered, "s—scented one."

"Scented one? I don't understand." And then he caught the slight fragrance too; the one that always set his employer off. Jasmine. It came from a heavily perfumed young woman, one half of the arm-in-arm couple passing in front of the car. Geoffrey rushed to shut the vents of the idling vehicle, selected to have the air inside recirculated instead of pulling it in from outside.

In the meantime, Richard sat with a scream lodged in his throat. Geoffrey draped his crucifix down the back of his shirt and pulled Richard in at once and held him until he calmed, like a parent comforting a child or, as a patrolling officer saw it, like two lovers gunning for a public lewdness citation. A rap at the window forced the two apart.

Geoffrey let the window's glass down. A flashlight's beam filled the car, illuminating both men in totality. "This is a public park."

"Just enjoying the river view, officer," Geoffrey said.

"See to it that's all you're enjoying."

"Yes, sir," the butler said, raising the window's glass back up.

Richard stared ahead, much more composed. "Do you know anything about what happened before I ended up here?"

"Yes. But what there is to tell might be a bit disconcerting. Are you sure you're ready to hear it?"

Richard nodded. "I am."

And so, Geoffrey told him everything that Penny had shared, not leaving anything out.

Richard's eyes closed. He rubbed hard at the bridge of his nose. "This is a nightmare. Cassie didn't deserve what you say happened to her. All she's done is help Ceese and me. If I'm not mistaken, I'm quite fond of Cassie."

Geoffrey recalled the conversation a few days back when Richard shared his new-found feelings for Cassie, acting like a nervous schoolboy crushing for the first time. "Indeed, it seems you are."

"Do you think she'll even talk to me once we get back so I could try and explain things to her even though I don't understand it myself."

"I certainly believe it's worth a shot, sir."

* * *

A flashlight's beam searched the ground behind the pub; it stopped on one of two empty blood pouches. Seconds later, a hand retrieved both from the pavement.

* * *

Penny stepped in front of Cassie like a protective mother bear. "No, absolutely not, Geoffrey. You weren't there when he attacked Cassie. I will not allow him to come in here and upset her all over again. It's not enough that he doesn't recall what happened. Let him figure it out first. It's just too dangerous."

Her voice carried into the hall. Richard heard and stepped into the parlor.

138

Cyn No More

"Why don't you ask Cassie what she wants?"

Cassie froze at the sight of him, but his voice worked to calm her. "It's all right, grandmother. "I want to hear what he has to say."

"All right, but you don't come any further into this room than where you are right now," Penny sternly told Richard.

"I don't know what to say," Richard started, "except that I don't remember what happened. Geoffrey filled me in on what he had been told, but that's all I know about the matter. I vaguely recall going to my coffin this morning. I do remember a little bit about our time in New York, though. All your help. You didn't deserve whatever happened to you earlier, and I wish I could take it back. But you know how the saying goes, 'if wishes were thrushes, then beggars would eat birds.'"

Unimpressed, Penny spoke up. "That's your idea of an apology? You nearly killed my granddaughter earlier, and you come in here spouting ancient English proverbs."

His eyes still trained on Cassie, he added, "I hope you can find it in your heart to forgive the Richard you knew in New York."

"I'm not sure I can, at least not right now anyway and especially since I don't understand what's going on. But I will think about it."

Sue Dent

Richard gave her as much of a smile as he could. "That's all I ask."

The two left, and Penny walked with Cassie to her room. "Are you sure you want to sleep in here after what happened earlier? There are other rooms."

"It's fine. Geoffrey had someone repair the balcony door and had crosses hung at each entrance. She pointed at the one on the door behind them. "And I have mine on now."

"Well, I won't force you to sleep elsewhere so long as it's your decision."

Penny turned to walk away but stopped at Cassie's question. "Do you think he meant it, what he said?"

Penny nodded. "As much as he could. He is a vampire again, though. Emotion is hard to come by."

And then came a troubling thought that Penny kept to herself. *And sometimes, so is the truth.*

* * *

Penny found Geoffrey in the pantry, where he treated Rodney's wound earlier. "You want to talk about what happened to your neck?"

He wiped it with antiseptic and applied a band-aid. "Shall we talk about it over tea?" A kettle whistled behind them.

Cyn No More

Sitting around the small dinette in the kitchen, Penny stirred honey into her brew. "So, Richard left here and headed into town?"

"He emailed me from a pub on the Thames. Asked me to bring him blood."

"Geoffrey, you're a wonderful butler, but you're a terrible liar. What are you leaving out?"

"Nothing that I plan on sharing."

"All right. I get that. He's your employer, not me. But why the offer of tea if you had nothing to share?"

"You've been with Master Richard for a very long time, before and after I was first employed by him."

"And not a day goes by that I don't hear something wonderful about Geoffrey." The comment should have brought a reaction but not a worried frown. "What is it?"

"Do you know why Master Richard reacts with such terror at the faintest scent of Jasmine?"

"I just know that he won't allow it to be planted anywhere around him. I suggested it once for his gardens, and I was never met with more resistance. Terror, you say?"

"His reaction to a woman wearing jasmine perfume earlier this evening—let's just say, I've never seen anyone look more terrified."

Penny sipped at her tea. "This morning, when we went to talk to Meri about Richard being a vampire again, he said something very interesting. He said Cyn was one of the two who cursed Richard, but she used to go by another name. She used to go by Jasmine. According to Meri, Richard, and Jasmine were betrothed. Clearly, it was all just a ruse to stay close to Richard until the night she could take him."

The butler sighed deep. "What are we dealing with?

"I don't know, Geoffrey, but I think the two of us need to work together to figure it out—for Richard's sake."

"Agreed."

"You can start by telling me about those scratches on your neck."

Chapter 23

THE FOLLOWING MORNING, Geoffrey patiently waited for Rodney to wake. At ten-thirty, the young man still slept. Not willing to wait any longer, Geoffrey stopped in front of Rodney's bedroom door with a small stack of washed clothes and knocked. He heard a moan and took it as an invitation to enter. He switched on a nearby lamp and called out to the Rodney sized lump under the covers. "I could use your assistance."

Undecipherable mumbling prompted Geoffrey to remove the pillow that covered the young man's head. "I beg your pardon, but were those words meant for me?"

Rodney pushed the covers aside and rolled to the edge of the bed. Sitting up, he said, "that's probably not a question you want to ask. Do you know what time it is?"

Geoffrey glanced at his watch. "It's precisely ten-thirty-two. Assuming you went straight to bed yesterday morning, then you've been resting for nearly twelve-hours."

"And because of this, you feel comfortable coming in here and waking me up?"

Sue Dent

"As I stated a moment ago, I need your help."

"I already have a toilet to unclog," Rodney said with a pained expression, "or did you forget that?"

"I've put that task to someone else."

"Well, put this new task to someone else."

"There is no one else.

Rodney wore a look of exasperation. "Do you mean to tell me that in this vast 'Wayne Manoresque' castle, with all its servants, you couldn't find anyone else to help you?"

"Ah, I see. Wayne Manor. In light of that comparison, wouldn't Batman always choose Robin to help him despite the number of others who would willingly assist?"

A strangled half-laugh left Rodney's throat. "No, you don't," he said, grabbed his pants from where Geoffrey set them down. Stepping into them, he said, "You don't get to be Batman." He pulled one of two shirts over his head. "Alfred, maybe." He put on the other shirt. "But not Batman."

They left the room together, stepped out of a side door and onto the drive that ran beside the castle. Even in the daylight, the place had a sinister vibe to it that Rodney couldn't seem to shake. Apprehensive, Rodney spoke up. "You didn't say anything about going outside."

Cyn No More

A wolf howled, and Rodney jogged the few steps he had fallen behind to catch up to Geoffrey. "Don't they ever turn the spooky off around here? Wolves aren't supposed to howl during the day."

Geoffrey stopped in front of the outbuilding at the end of the drive; its four garage doors shut. He moved to the far right one and produced a set of keys. He used one to unlock the door, then slid it up. Looking over Geoffrey's shoulder, Rodney reacted with deadpan enthusiasm. "Oh look, another coffin."

Geoffrey moved toward it, pulled a handkerchief from a pocket, and wiped at the closed top in spite of it being polished and spotless already. Speaking quietly, as though respectful of the dead, he said, "It's my father's coffin."

As though being chased by something terrifying, Rodney backpedaled until he slammed into the wall behind him. More than a few tools hanging there fell and clanged to the concrete floor. The butler spun around. One last tool clanged down.

"Y—your father's in there?" Rodney stuttered.

"Are you quite mad? My father isn't in there. The coffin is empty." Geoffrey creaked the lid open as proof. Rodney cautiously approached and peeked inside. "I just need you to help me move it to the basement."

"Because three coffins in the basement are better than two?"

145

"At last count, we had three vampires."

"Right. And I understand that vampires need coffins—because of the lure—or something. But they don't need basements. There are no windows here. Why not just leave it?"

Geoffrey's face grew uncharacteristically tense. "Master Rodney, does the thought of manual labor bother you that much?"

"Just unnecessary manual labor." To Geoffrey's strained look, he added, "and why are you lugging your father's coffin around anyway? Empty or not, that's just weird."

"I'll only tell you if you promise to hold your reaction, or over-reaction, until after I'm done speaking."

"I'll try."

"My father *is* a vampire."

Rodney's eyes widened. "You're not going to make this easy, are you?"

"Not to worry, he isn't around anymore. I keep his coffin close should he return." Geoffrey's tone turned melancholy. "I looked after him for quite a few years."

"The way you look after Richard now?"

Cyn No More

"Yes, and the way I looked after Richard in the past as well. Before my father was a vampire, he was an excellent carpenter."

Rodney spied a label on the inside of the coffin lid. "W. T. F. Geoffrey & Son Ltd.," he read aloud. "Seriously? W-T-F-G?"

"William Thaddius Francis Geoffrey," the butler said innocuously. "My Father's name and mine as well. Is there something funny about that?"

"Um, no," Rodney said. "It's a lovely name. Good name. Good solid name. Your dad made this then," Rodney said, turned back to the coffin.

"Yes, he built coffins for many years and then, without any warning, he left and, I don't know where he went or why. A few years later, Master Richard hired me on because of my experience with vampires. He used my father's coffin then." Geoffrey had that wistful look again. "It seems a lifetime ago. I suppose I'm just hoping my father will return someday to explain why he left. But that's why I carry his coffin around, to have something to remind me of him, and I'd prefer to have it in the basement now that it can be used."

"Okay," Rodney acknowledged. "Why are we standing around then? Let's move it to the basement."

The church-truck made the task doable. Halfway across the lawn, however, Rodney needed to catch his breath and called for rest. Geoffrey took the

147

opportunity to come out of his butler's coat and overshirt because the day had warmed up nicely.

Rodney gawked at the butler's muscled arms and the toned chest and abs hinted at by his t-shirt. "You needed my help moving this?"

Geoffrey's eyes glinted humor, a welcome expression, Rodney decided, after their last conversation. "I can't very well push and steer at the same time now, can I."

"Ha! Ha! But all kidding aside, you didn't get that fit being a butler."

"I was once a soldier in the Queen's army. I never gave up the habit of working out and eating right. You know, with regular exercise and a healthy—"

"Forget it," Rodney said, cutting the butler off and standing. "Not interested. I'm fine just the way I am."

Break over; they pushed the coffin along and into the servant's corridors, where the smooth floor enabled them to move more quickly. Still, Rodney called for one more break.

"I hope your dad's worth all this," he said, leaned against the casket and its four-wheel roller.

"Yours wouldn't be?"

He choked back a laugh. "My ol' man is a drunk bum who took custody of me when I was five so he wouldn't have to pay child support. He rates low on my worth-meter."

"He did take care of you, though. That should count for something."

"Yeah, he smacked me around when I didn't bring him his beer fast enough, which was pretty much every time."

"Did he drink often?"

"I think you mean was he ever sober?"

"I see."

"Once I learned he was easy to outrun when he was drunk; things were easier. I'm not complaining. Others had it worse."

"Master Josh," Geoffrey assumed.

"Yeah, his step-dad was brutal. Couldn't deal with Josh's mixed heritage. Threatened to beat the 'white' out of him and tried regularly. I let Josh hang out at my hell hole of a home most of the time until he found his way—and sadly, drugs. Claimed they helped him cope, but then he started to abuse them." Rodney stopped talking when he realized he'd said more than he meant to. "Dude, this is just between you and me, right?"

"You have my word."

No further breaks were required, and, with the church truck at the level of the coffin-stand, easing it over only took a few quick seconds.

"Thank you for your help, Master Rodney," Geoffrey said appreciatively. "And to show my gratitude at your understanding my reasoning for bringing the coffin here, I'm relieving you of any further obligation to me."

Rodney jerked his head around, studied the butler's face. "What? No more chores?"

"No more chores. You can pay me when you get the money. No pressure."

Rodney turned sideways to leave but hesitated. "You ever try looking for your dad?"

"I never stop looking."

Rodney nodded. "I hope you find him."

Chapter 24

THERE HAD BEEN SO little free time over the past few days that Penny took advantage. She headed to the bookshelf behind Richard's desk, felt for and triggered the latch she knew to be there, and pushed the bookcase-door open enough for her to slide through.

She followed the steps down, entered the required combination into the keypad on the wall, and went inside the environmentally controlled room that housed her organized collection of diaries. Richard worked tirelessly to prepare the room for her, understanding how much her writings meant to her. She had never seen him work quite as hard at anything before or since.

Prompted by her vision, she took out several diaries from around the time when she first met Richard and stared stunned when she found a bookmark in one of them. She kept that one out and put the others back.

She recognized the bookmark. It was from a collection she had given Richard on one of his many birthdays—only a few years ago.

Sue Dent

With tentative fingers, she opened the diary to the marked page and saw that it was the day, the exact day that she met Richard.

And there was more.

She dropped into a nearby chair certain that her legs would not hold her and read from a note placed inside, written by Richard's hand.

"He is mine now."

* * *

As the sun descended toward the horizon, Ceese searched for Penny. She found Cassie instead, her bedroom door open. Cassie looked up from her reading; one of quite a few books Penny gave her on metaphysics and second sight. "Do you need something?" *Is that even a possibility?*

"I was looking for Penny," Ceese admitted. "But maybe you can help."

Cassie put the book down. *Don't look too eager*, she told herself. "I'll certainly try."

Ceese walked over and lifted her shirt to reveal a bruise on the lower left side of her abdomen. "Henderson put something in me. I can feel it."

Cassie waited for permission to explore the area and prodded with gentle fingers. "You're looking for

Cyn No More

Penny then, and you want me to help you find her so she can take whatever that is out?"

"Unless you can take it out."

Suspicious but willing to play along to earn the teen's trust, she left to get Richard's medical bag. Richard had become a doctor through online classes to make it easier to get blood. He kept a medical bag around for appearances; in case anyone asked.

Cassie found a scalpel inside and some numbing cream. She instructed Ceese to lay on her bed and applied antiseptic. Giving the cream time to work, she cut and removed four small cylinder-shaped pellets she found.

Penny passed the open door, returned, and did a double-take. "What in the world?"

Cassie placed a Band-Aid on the small incision and said, "Ceese was looking for you but found me instead. Henderson injected these pellets under her skin. I'm going to find Kyle to see if he can identify them."

"I saw him in the parlor," Penny shared. Before she left to follow Cassie, she turned to Ceese. "Did you come to her for help, or was she just a convenient alternative?" Ceese's unwillingness to answer forced a disappointed frown onto Penny's face. "We'll talk about this later."

Sue Dent

***

Kyle was rarely any help. But he was majoring in pharmaceuticals and had learned a lot working in his father's lab. On the computer in the parlor and wearing earbuds, Cassie tapped him on the shoulder.

"Don't bug me. I'm in the middle of a campaign!" He moved the mouse radically around.

"Can you tell me what these are?" Cassie asked, opening her hand to reveal what she held.

He didn't respond.

Penny walked over and yanked at the cord of one earbud. She had his attention. "I can put a password on this computer."

Kyle rolled his eyes and looked at what Cassie held. "They're hormone pellets. This one is testosterone, and the others look like estradiol. Can I get back to my game now?" He stuffed the earbud back in his ear.

"Why would Henderson implant hormone pellets?"

"I don't know," Penny said, equally perplexed. "But, the implications are certainly frightening."

***

Penny found Ceese in her room, sitting cross-legged on the bed. Penny sat down to face her. "Those were

154

hormone pellets Cassie took out for you. Do you have any idea what Henderson was planning?"

Ceese shook her head back and forth. "What are hormones? Will they hurt me?"

Deciding a lecture on hormone pharmaceuticals would only confuse her more, Penny said, "No, but I do want to discuss your interaction with Cassie earlier. She's very excited that you turned to her for help. Should she be?"

"I didn't turn to her. I was looking for you."

"I knew better. Ceese, why won't you give my granddaughter a chance?"

"She isn't your granddaughter."

"A few greats do not change that she and I are related, just the relationship."

Ceese shrugged nonchalantly. "She reminds me of George."

Stunned at hearing her late husband's name, she asked, "What in the world does George have to do with this?"

"He was weak."

"He grew to be strong, Ceese. You only knew him for a short time. You could've known him longer if you had stayed that day instead of running off the way you did, making me believe a wolf attacked you. It was quite a few months before I sensed you were alive. At any rate, you need to give Cassie a chance to prove she is strong as well."

"The weak never survive in the pack. Do you know what happens to the weakest member?"

"Stop right there. This isn't a pack, and we're not talking about wolves. We're talking about my granddaughter. Now, I know it's hard, but you're going to have to adjust to being mortal again. Promise me you'll try harder to do that."

"I promise."

As soon as Penny left the room, Ceese had an itch. And without giving it a thought, she moved a leg and scratched like a dog.

Chapter 25

TWILIGHT GAVE WAY TO the inky darkness of a moonless night. Richard felt fortunate to have located a small deer so quickly. He felt less than fortunate at the sudden scent of Jasmine on the breeze, and the words, "hello, pet," whispered seductively in his ear.

He closed his eyes tightly against what he knew would follow; a tongue teasing, sharp points of fangs pressing, a nightmare from long ago returned.

"Miss me? I know I've missed you. So much so that I had to get your daddy to help me find you." She moved around to face him. Dark hair framed a seductive face, full lips pouted. "But because your daddy did what he did, I can't have you completely." She drew a curved nail slowly down his lips dragging the bottom one along before letting it go. "But because of what I did, I can still have my fun with you."

He braced for the pain that would follow even though it wouldn't matter.

It never mattered.

* * *

Sue Dent

Landscaping lights lit the front lawn. Rodney saw Ceese staring into the forest of trees on one side of the castle.

"Hey," he said, came to stand beside her. "I saw you from the—um—window." An awkward silence followed, and it became more awkward when Rodney realized, all at once, that he had nothing else to add to the conversation. He winged it. "Just thought I'd come to say hey. I heard a wolf howl out here earlier this afternoon."

"I'm not afraid of wolves," she said.

He sighed when she didn't say more. "Yeah. Right." Why was she making small-talk so difficult? "Is everything okay?"

"Yes. Why?"

"Because I just thought that with Zade gone and you learning that your dad was your real dad—well, I guess I just thought you might be in higher spirits," *and more excited to see me since I initiated the DNA test that proved Meri was your biological father and not Zade.*

She continued to stare. "I'm fine," and then, "do you think Joachim's out there? I mean, do you think he's close by?"

Cyn No More

Rodney couldn't pin down the reason why he didn't like her longing tone whenever she mentioned the werewolf. "To be honest, I hope not."

A human cry distracted. A wolf howled

"That's Richard," Ceese said and took off running.

Rodney called after her. "Hey, come back. Let's get help." He looked toward the castle. But if he didn't follow her now, he would lose her. "Wait up."

She couldn't run like a wolf anymore, so Rodney had that going for him. "Whoa," he said, coming up on the scene, Richard laying on the ground, his body wracked by spasms, his face a mask of pain.

Ceese stared, eyes glazed. "He's dying."

"What makes you think that? I mean, it's obviously not his best day, but I don't think he's dying."

"I know what a cursed being looks like when they're dying. Zade made me watch Joachim after he—" She choked back emotion.

"Come on," Rodney said in a calming voice, "nobody's gonna die." Getting on the ground, he placed his arms around Richard, pulled him in tight, and made shushing noises; all the things he did to ease Josh through withdrawal. And like Josh, Richard calmed.

"See," Rodney said at the accomplishment. "Now, let's get him back to the castle before he starts up again."

* * *

Penny was at her bedroom door, having decided to turn in early when she heard the echo of the large front door closing and the shuffling of footsteps.

She walked back to the main hall, rounded the corner, and gawked at what she saw; Rodney and Ceese struggling to carry Richard between them as he jerked and thrashed about like someone in the throes of death. "What on earth?"

"We were hoping you could tell us," Rodney said as they laid him on the couch.

Ceese added, "This is how we found him—in the woods. I heard him cry out after a wolf howled."

There was nothing to suggest he'd been attacked by a wolf, though. There was, however, blood on the front of Rodney's shirt, Penny noticed. "Are you bleeding?"

Rodney followed her stare and looked at what she'd referenced with a nod. "That must be from when I tried to quiet him so we could carry him here."

"You held him?"

"Yeah."

Cyn No More

"His back to you?"

"Sort of, yeah."

Penny reached down and turned Richard's head slightly, gasped. "Fresh bite marks."

"I told you he was dying," Ceese said to Rodney.

"Two cursed beings," Penny muttered.

Behind them in the main hall, the front door opened and closed. "Move," Meri said, rushed into the parlor. Those standing around backed away at his urgent tone. Quick steps took him to the couch. He settled on the edge, and covered the fresh toothy imprints with the palm of his right hand, sat in thoughtful repose as if meditating. Richard stopped thrashing and crying out. Meri finally took his hand back and slumped forward, his head hanging heavy.

Chapter 26

UNCERTAIN OF WHAT JUST happened, Penny asked. "Is he dead?"

A few seconds later, Meri found the strength to answer. "He's not dead. Cyn would never kill him and certainly not at the risk of dying herself."

"You're saying that Cyn did this, but no curse was transferred?"

"You see where the marks are. She was feeding off his essence."

"Yes, I see," Penny remarked. "She did choose a lesser vein. But Meri, I've known enough vampires in my time to understand that feeding off someone's essence, while possible, is hardly worth the effort. Why is she doing this to him?"

He looked up. "I guess there's no reason not to tell you now."

"I'm listening."

"There are those whose essence is worth taking. For instance, the firstborn of a high-ranking member of the *daoine maithe*."

Cyn No More

"Of which Richard isn't," Penny said to a look that told her she was wrong. "How Meri?"

"Julia is; therefore, Richard is as well. They share an essence that is highly intoxicating to those who can consume it."

"Okay," Penny said at the first hint as to why Cyn was hell-bent on having Richard. "But it seems odd that Cyn wouldn't go after Julia too."

Meri wore a look of distress and even guilt. "She did. That's where this all started. Julia was eighteen. I was so much in love with her. One day I saw a number of the *daoine maithe* gathered on the banks of the river. I went to investigate and found Julia floating there, drowned. Later I learned she had jumped in to escape Cyn. But she couldn't swim. The *daoine maithe* said they would return her to me if I promised to protect her. I swore that I would. Shortly after we wed, Cyn tried again. I returned home from the mission to find her holding Julia at the end of her fangs. Julia was pregnant with Richard, and she begged me to save him. I promised Cyn she could have our firstborn if she just let Julia go."

"And Julia was okay with this?"

"She knew it was all talk. Knew I would never turn Richard over to Cyn."

Sue Dent

Penny went back over the story in her mind and had a question for Meri. "You say she jumped in the river to get away from Cyn?"

"Yes."

"What river?"

"The *Abhainn Dubh.* The Black River. The River Forth."

"Why would she do that?"

"I can't say that I know."

"Deen-eh My-heh," Rodney sounded out. "I know what that means. I took "Folklore and Mythology" in my first semester at Templeton." He turned to Ceese, "It means your mother's a fairy."

Seconds after he spoke, an invisible force lifted Rodney off the ground and flipped him in midair. Ceese looked at him on the floor. "They don't like to be called that."

At once, Meri turned toward Ceese. "They're here? You can see them?" She nodded. "Of course, you're the seventh born."

"So are you, Meri," Penny said, confused.

"The vampire's evil won't allow me to see them."

* * *

Cyn No More

The cave echoed her rage as Cyn called out. "Where is she?"

The *daoine maithe* imprisoned by her evil nearly a century ago huddled closer together. They cringed when Cyn targeted a fey near the front of the group. It shrieked in pain from the surge of evil forced upon it.

"Come out now, or I will show this one no mercy." The threat worked. A thin mist turned up the one she sought. Cyn released the fey from her grip. "You led her to where I was before I could finish." Tears welled in the eyes of the one she accused. "I will not tolerate your betrayal too. I will get what I want, whether you like it or not. I will take your son, and if you do not cooperate in the future, I will kill the one you call 'husband' as well. Never forget that you are my prisoner. You will do as told—or I will kill them all."

* * *

"What does Cyn want with the *daoine maithe*?" Penny asked.

"With their help, she can achieve ethereal form, possess Richard, and she can force him to do things he wouldn't otherwise do."

Penny nodded. "Well, that explains a lot."

Meri turned to Ceese and Rodney. "It's good you found him when you did. Otherwise, he'd be with Cyn now. But how did you find him as Cyn isn't that easy to locate when she's up to no good?"

"I followed Ceese," Rodney said.

Ceese held onto her response for a long moment and then said, "I followed Mother."

Chapter 27

MICHELLE'S ALARM CLOCK RANG out. She rolled across her bed to silence it. She had set it for 8:00 AM but didn't need to be at work until four that afternoon. She had things to do. She dressed, took up one of the blood pouches from the alley, and studied the label for information, anything that would help her locate the dispatch center. There was a phone number. She called it, relied on her natural cunning to get the courier's name. "Two can play at this game," she said, thinking of the butler from the night before.

A half-hour later, Michelle stood in front of the courier's door and knocked. No one answered. She knocked again and said, "Mr. O'Keefe, I want to talk to you about one of your deliveries. I promise I won't take up much of your time." Still no response. "I have whiskey."

She heard movement, and the door opened a crack. She held a bottle of Bushmills for him to see. The door closed; the chain lock unfastened.

"The name's Danny," he said, taking the bottle from her. "Close the door behind you." He cleared a space on a cluttered couch so she could sit, then fell back into the well-worn chair he vacated to answer the door. He opened the whiskey, poured himself a shot, and threw it back. "What do you want to know?"

She wasn't surprised to hear an Irish accent. She suspected as much by the last name. "I was wondering if you could give me the address of your last delivery?"

He shook his head, vigorously back and forth. "You got no business having that address or going out there. None at all. And I won't be giving it to you."

"Was it that delivery that made you quit your job?"

He took a second. Poured and threw back another shot. "No. Not exactly. Maybe. No matter the answer, I'm not giving up the address. That castle is no good. I'll not be the one to send you there. If it means you take your whiskey back with you, so be it."

Her eyes scanned the coffee-table top in front of the couch as he spoke. He said the word 'castle' and her eyes fell on the picture of one on the cover of a tabloid magazine partially covered by other tabloids. She thought fast. "I tell you what. I'll leave the whiskey if you let me take a few of those *Sunday Sports* off your hands. It's my mum," she convincingly lied, "she loves to read them. Just doesn't like to be seen buying them."

He stiffened.

Cyn No More

She held her composure.

"Take what you want," he said after an uncertain moment.

Once outside, and nearly a block away, she trashed all but the one with the photograph of the castle.

* * *

Rodney and Kyle followed Marissa's terrified gaze over to the small dinette.

"What's he doing out of his coffin?" Kyle asked Rodney.

"There's only one way to find out."

Rodney walked over and sat. "Do you know what time it is, Josh?"

"It's breakfast time," Josh replied, sloppily spooning sugary 'O's drowned in milk out of a bowl and shoving them into his mouth.

"Mm-hmm," Rodney said like a parent speaking to a young child. "That's right. But something's wrong with this picture. Do you know what it is?"

Josh struck a thoughtful pose. "I'm not a vampire anymore?"

"That's right," Rodney said with a smile. "And can you explain that?"

In between bites, Josh laid out his reasoning. "I was in my coffin yesterday morning, and I saw Henderson about to curse this kind of chubby dude—you know in my head. Kinda like I was watching a movie."

Cassie, having joined Kyle and Penny in the doorway and triggered by Josh's last comment, said, "You mean the way Richard said he saw Henderson try to curse that homeless man back in New York."

Josh turned, hesitated before answering then said, "Yeah, I guess."

"And you stopped him," Penny added.

"Yeah," he said, going back to his cereal.

Rodney left Josh to his breakfast and met with the others in the hall. "So, he's cured?"

"It is one selfless-act," Penny said, "albeit a pretty weak one."

"It didn't work to cure Richard," Cassie said, "when Richard stopped Henderson from cursing that homeless man."

"Yes, but Josh hasn't been a vampire nearly as long. Those freshly turned often have an easier time of it."

Kyle responded with utter glee and pumped a fist in the air. "Yes! Josh isn't a vampire anymore, so we can take him and leave this haunted mansion."

Cyn No More

Ceese walked up. "You can't leave," she said to Rodney. "We still have to help Richard. And Father too."

"Not our concern," Kyle chirped. "Right, Rodney? You said it yourself. We're only here for Josh."

"Yeah, that's what I said—"

Kyle whipped out his cell phone. "Great, I'll book a flight back now."

"Hold up," Rodney replied, covered the screen of the phone with his hand. "That's what I said, but—" Geoffrey walked out of the kitchen. Rodney grabbed him by the arm "—but G-man has me working off what I owe him in chores." The butler's face was one big question mark. "And so, I can't leave until I've paid him back. Right, G-man?"

All eyes were on the butler now, and he did not disappoint. "Master Rodney, if you're so intent on paying me back, then why have you not started weeding the front flower bed as I asked you to?"

"Weeding," Rodney nodded, "right. I'm on it."

A disgruntled Kyle followed.

Josh overheard from the kitchen and bolted after his friends. "Did somebody say weed? Wait up."

Penny turned to Geoffrey. "You heard all of that about Josh, then."

"I did."

"If Henderson is out there recklessly cursing others and succeeds, there will be all sorts of curious people about. What if the courier that Josh saved, talks?"

Geoffrey could take a hint. Having folks nosing around could be very risky for his employer. "Perhaps I should go into town and have a chat with the man. Offer a monetary settlement for his silence."

"I think that would be wise for all involved."

* * *

Traffic was surprisingly light.

Geoffrey got the man's address and pulled up to the courier's home and parked across the street. He made a move to get out but stopped short at seeing a familiar face, Michelle, from the night before exiting, the residence.

172

Chapter 28

MARISSA, LEAVING BRENDAN'S ROOM, and carrying a full tray of food, passed Penny in the hall.

"Is that Brendan's breakfast?" Penny asked before she could get by.

"Yes, ma'am, he said he's not hungry and to take it away—unless you'd rather I take it back to him."

"He's awake?"

"Yes, ma'am."

"I suppose you should take it back to the kitchen, but give me a few minutes with him before you return to your duties."

His eyes were open, but he didn't respond when she said his name. "You sent Marissa back with your breakfast. Why?"

"I nae want it, and I nae want her here."

"I need someone here to let me know if you try to get up on that broken ankle. Therefore, she's staying." She softened her tone. "But how did you break it, Brendan?" He turned his head away. "I want to thank you for saving Cassie."

"I wish brother had killed me."

173

Sue Dent

"You don't mean that, Brendan."

He followed that up with a very hollow, "Please, let me be."

* * *

After knocking and getting no answer, Darrell inserted his copy of Cassie's apartment key into the lock of her apartment door and let himself in. It had been two weeks, and she hadn't returned any of his calls or texts, and now he had some information he knew she would want.

"Cassie," he called out. He flipped a switch, but the room remained dark. Too dark. It was early afternoon and a very sunny day outside. The room shouldn't be black as pitch. Using the flashlight on his phone, he searched around. He found the windows and sliding glass door treated with aluminum foil and nothing in the refrigerator but a few cans of beer. There were a few things on the kitchen table; a syringe an empty vial. The latter, he slipped in a pocket. He also found a piece of paper with flight information and something else.

* * *

Goat-herder Peter Drummond drunk-walked toward the lean-to behind his small cabin; his home before the wolves, summoned by Bastóne and that girl with the wolf-eyes, arrived and despoiled it of any dignity, leaving it a metaphoric fleshless carcass and a terrifying reminder of what happened that evening.

Cyn No More

The goat-herder upended the bottle he carried with him and drained it of its content. He used to drink for pleasure; now, he drank to forget. The bottle empty, he tossed it aside, dropped unceremoniously to the ground, and crab-crawled beneath the cover of his shelter.

A sudden tug at each pant leg roused him, and he bellowed vociferously and drunkenly thinking perhaps that the wolves were back. The tugging stopped, and the goat-herder squinted with bloodshot eyes through a crack in his shelter at an unclothed man presently walking in a tight circle, muttering, "Too loud. Too loud."

The goat-herder grew quiet as he watched, and the clothes thief took advantage. He rushed the lean-to and with one final yank, pulled the goat-herders pants off and ran.

* * *

"Hey," Kyle said, clutching a ripped-from-the-ground plant in his hand, "isn't that the butler?"

A car pulled into the drive and came to an abrupt halt. Geoffrey got out and stared, his form stiff, his expression rigid.

"Oh snap," Kyle remarked, "it is the butler, and he doesn't look happy. I'm outtie." He dropped the plant and ran, Josh not far behind.

Sue Dent

Rodney stood from where he knelt. Dirt covered his hands. A worried look covered his face. "Don't look at me like that, G-man."

With great restraint, Geoffrey said, "I thought you understood that the chore of weeding wasn't a real chore."

"Yeah, I figured. But then, Kyle followed me. And then, Josh. What was I supposed to do? I had to make it look real, or they would've known the truth—that I wanted to stay even if Josh wasn't cursed."

"So, in turn, you and your friends uproot every plant in the bed?"

Rodney shrugged. "I don't know what a weed looks like G-man. All these plants, they look the same." The butler's brows drew in even closer. "Okay, fine. Don't believe me. But at least you can see I'm trying to fix things." Rodney gestured with both hands at his pathetic effort; one plant stuck haphazardly in the ground.

"That, Master Rodney, is a weed."

Rodney dropped his hands to his sides. "Do you need more proof. I told you I didn't know the difference."

The butler came out of his coat, laid it across a nearby garden bench, rolled up his sleeves.

Rodney took an alarmed step back. "You're gonna fight me over this?"

176

Cyn No More

Geoffrey sighed. "As you pointed out a moment ago, I am also partially responsible for this debacle. So together, we will 'fix things.'"

It took the remainder of the suddenly cloudy afternoon.

* * *

Thickening clouds proceeded the dismal dusk. Light rain and an occasional rumble of thunder hinted at impending storms. Henderson left his cave hideaway straight away to avoid mucking about in the mud for a meal. His pre-rain hunt took him to the top of a hill. He rustled through a few ground squirrel dens but scented a much bigger prize. He levitated toward it and landed softly behind his dread-headed nemesis, Josh; the one who shot him effectively, helping Ceese escape from his basement lab, also the one who threw him into a tree the evening before and the one who robbed him of a human meal.

"Well, well, well," he said. "Out feeding?"

Josh jerked surprise and then collected himself. "Henderson—dude. No, I don't have to do that anymore. I'm not a vampire. I'm cured."

Lifting a curious brow, Henderson said, "Oh? Do tell."

"It had something to do with keeping you from cursing that delivery guy."

"Yes. You deprived me of a nice meal."

Sue Dent

"Yeah, I guess I did," Josh said, suddenly sorry he had brought that up. "You're not gonna curse me again, are you?"

"The thought crossed my mind, but honestly, you're more trouble to me as a vampire." And he could do so much more damage with Josh as a mortal and an addict. "Tell you what? I'm about to go into town. A taxi will be here shortly. Why don't you come with me? It'll be like old times. Maybe I can find you a little something to help you celebrate."

Josh's eyes brightened. "Yeah?"

"Sure," Henderson said, watching the cab pull up to the designated mile-marker. He opened a back door and said, "after you."

* * *

A heavy rain fell throughout dinner, the first real meal in at least a day for those presently sitting around the table.

"Where's Josh?" Penny asked, noting his absence. "I'm surprised not to see him here."

"Who cares," Kyle said, talking around a roll stuffed in his mouth. "Without him here, there's more food for me."

"He was with you earlier," Rodney said, a concerned edge to his voice.

"Yeah. Well, he's somewhere else now."

178

Cyn No More

Meri walked in on their speculating. "I know where he is. I just saw him get into a car with Henderson."

Rodney froze, his hand mid-way to his mouth with a fork-full of food. "Are you sure that's what you saw?"

"As sure as I see you sitting there. It was a taxi. They both got in."

Rodney lowered the fork back to his plate.

"He went willingly?" Cassie asked.

Rodney answered. "Of course, he went willingly. He's not a vampire anymore. He's gone back to satisfying his other addiction. Henderson can get him what he needs, or at least that's what he thinks."

"Not a vampire?" Meri said.

Penny filled him in on what he'd missed, Josh's story, adding at the end, "Josh has been up all day, bustling around."

"That's good news, then," Meri said, not understanding Rodney's long face.

"Yeah, great news," Rodney unenthusiastically replied. "Now he's an addict again—and he's out with his supplier." He pinned Kyle with a hard look. "I thought I told you to keep an eye on him."

"Where's he gonna go? We're in the middle of nowhere."

Meri dismissed himself amid the harsh voices saying that he would keep an eye out for Josh.

Marissa replaced Meri in the doorway. "Ma'am," she said, addressing Penny. "I left Master Brendan's room to get his dinner tray, and when I returned, he was gone."

"Well, he couldn't have gotten far," Penny said, standing.

Chapter 29

HAVING SEARCHED ALL AROUND, Penny looked to the others, everyone from the dinner table who had joined the search. "Where could he have gone?" She looked at the end of his bed. "His boots are missing."

Geoffrey, coming in from outside, met them in the main hall, just as they were about to broaden their search. His faced etched with worry, he said, "Someone is standing at the top of the West Tower."

* * *

Fisting the excess fabric of Drummond's pants in hand, he paced, counted, and occasionally glanced up at the west tower a little over a hundred yards away. He would count to one hundred and twenty and start over again.

* * *

Josh stared at Henderson's back as the college professor negotiated with the employee at the Fed Ex store counter. "You'll send me a text once the package arrives? And you've got the correct number?" The employee rattled it back off to him. Seemingly satisfied, Henderson walked over to where Josh stood, put an arm around his shoulder. "Now, let's go take care of you, shall we?"

* * *

Lightning occasionally flashed, but the rain had stopped. The look of concern on Ceese's face at seeing Brendan perched to jump, pushed Rodney to act. "How do you get up there?" he asked Geoffrey.

"I suppose there are several ways. I'm guessing Master Brendan used the entrance to the servant's corridors in his room. Follow me."

Rodney jerked Kyle along by the arm. "Hey, you ever heard of asking?"

Geoffrey shoved at the door in Brendan's room. "It's jammed shut."

"He didn't want anyone stopping him," Rodney reasonably concluded. "Are there other entrances that lead to the tower?"

"They all should." They followed Geoffrey across the hall and into a furniture-less room. "This entrance," he said, opening another door, motioned toward a map on the wall, "comes complete with directions." He pointed. "This map shows where you are now. There should be plaques to lead you the rest of the way." Rodney took out his phone and snapped a picture of the map for future reference.

"Come on," Rodney said to Kyle.

Cyn No More

"Master Rodney," Geoffrey said to their backs, "remember what I told you about the corridors and do be careful."

"Careful?" Kyle said at the butler closing the door behind them. "What did he mean by that? What's there to be careful of? It's just a hallway, right?"

* * *

Henderson reached underneath Josh's thick dreads, yanked at the collar of his bomber jacket, and dragged him along until they both stood in the alley. "Wait here."

The young junkie Henderson spied, sat under cover of a worn cardboard box that dripped wet from the recent rain. He flicked at the spur of a lighter until it flamed steady and then heated the bottom of the spoon he held. Henderson waited until the cooked solution was drawn up into a syringe before he made his presence known.

He locked eyes with the junkie, worked quickly to hypnotize him. "I'll take that," he said, confiscating the goods.

Josh saw the junkie slump over onto his side, and when Henderson returned, he asked, "What did you do to him?"

"He's going to take a little nap, now. In the meantime, look at what I got for you." Henderson held out the syringe and tourniquet for Josh to take. "It will be just like old times."

Josh stared wide-eyed. "I'm pretty sure that's a speedball. I don't do speedballs."

Henderson puzzled over his words. "You seem picky for a drug addict."

"Speedball's are risky. They can kill you. Even I know that."

Henderson smiled tightly. "Take off your jacket."

"Come on," Josh whimpered through the hypnosis even as he complied, removed his jacket, placed the tourniquet around an arm, and tightened it.

"That's a good boy," Henderson said, handing Josh the syringe. He reveled in the street-punks pleading words even as he stuck the needle into a vein and pumped the plunger. Henderson's smile grew as Josh's eyes rolled back in his head.

* * *

"This way," Rodney yelled over his shoulder to prod Kyle, who lagged behind.

"I'm not blind. I can see you," but then Kyle nearly ran into Rodney when Rodney stopped short. "Hey, what's the big idea?"

There were two passages in front of them but no plaque to direct. "Flip a coin," Kyle suggested.

Cyn No More

"We can help you?" two girls said, one girl in each corridor.

Twins.

"Missy and Millicent," Rodney whispered. And they were just as Geoffrey described; dressed in period-piece dresses, looked to be around thirteen.

A look of disbelief covered Kyle's face. "You know them?"

"They're not real. They're ghosts."

"You're going to the West Tower," one said. "You need to go that way."

"Wow!" Kyle said. "Helpful ghost. How cool is that? C'mon Rodney let's get this over with," and he took off in the direction one girl suggested. Seconds later, Kyle howled in pain. "That's funny," he said, returning with a hand pressed to his forehead. "It's a dead-end—and too dark to see that the ceiling drops. You two are hysterical."

Kyle frowned at the girl's giggles.

Rodney smiled. "Thanks for saving me the trouble of deciding which one tells the truth," Rodney replied before heading off the other way.

"You know what," Kyle fumed from where he stood. "You can do this by yourself. I've had it." No response let him know Rodney could not hear him or simply refused to answer. Kyle stood alone with the ghost girls for all of two seconds. "Wait up. I'm coming."

Rodney climbed a set of stairs and came to a door standing open. He exited through it to see Brendan perched to jump.

Chapter 30

HENDERSON ATTEMPTED TO FLAG down a taxi with a stoned Josh at his side. He wanted to get him back to the castle, and back to Rodney, before the drugs wore off, or before Josh died; if a speedball affected the result that Josh indicated it might.

"Not a bloody chance he's getting in my cab," one driver said. "Clean him up and sober him up. After that, if you're not riding with him, I want an exact address and a phone number for him, plus yours. And there'll be an up-front soiling charge. He can have it back as long as he doesn't puke, shit, or piss himself. And if he can't get in his house, once at his destination, he'll be spending the night sitting on his doorstep. I'm not his mum, and I'm not social services."

* * *

Michelle's shift over, she looked at the address she had scribbled down earlier. She left the pub and stopped cold when she heard the same address spoken by someone nearby. She looked up to see a man in a tweed jacket talking to a cabbie.

Sue Dent

"I told you," the driver repeated, "unless you are riding with him, or someone else is riding with him, you'll need to sober him up first."

"Look, I'll pay you twice as much if you'll just take him as he is," the man in the tweed jacket said, waved several large bills as proof.

"Sober him up, and you've got a deal."

Michelle took advantage. "Oi," she called out, bumping past tweed-jacket-man and quickly wrapping an arm around the waist of the staggering, barely standing street punk next to him, saying, "why didn't you wait for me? I told you I'd take uh—I'm sorry, what was his name again?"

"Josh," tweed-jacket-man said, confused but happily playing along.

"Yeah. I told you I'd ride along with Josh and make sure he got back all right." She then guided the oblivious young man with the long dreads toward the cab and maneuvered him into the backseat. She then got in herself and pulled the door shut.

With one quick motion, and before tweed-jacket-man changed his mind, the now cooperative cabbie grabbed the wad of bills and said, "deal." He then climbed into his cab and sped away from the curb.

The sudden movement pushed Josh over onto Michelle. She shoved him off. The rubber tourniquet tied loosely on his arm, fell to his wrist. She tried, too

188

late, to cover it. The driver saw her quick movements in the rear-view mirror and applied the brake. Both she and Josh jerked forward.

"None of that in here," the man said, turning in his seat. "I'll put ya both out."

Michelle quickly untied the tourniquet and removed it. "It's not what you think." She dumped the limited contents of her purse in plain view as proof that she wasn't hiding anything. She turned any pockets inside out as well. "Nothing here either. No drugs."

"As long as we're clear," the cabbie said.

She put her hands up. "We're clear."

* * *

Kyle ran after Rodney and up the stairs to the open door at the top. Seeing Brendan poised to jump, and Rodney halfway to him, he yelled, "so, what's the plan?"

Brendan jerked his head around, saw Rodney set to lunge toward him and over the edge he went.

* * *

Those on the ground drew a collective breath. Not one of them noticed the one running from the woods until Brendan landed safely and solidly in his arms; the stranger's pants pooling at his feet as he released his hold on them to catch Brendan.

"One hundred and twenty," the fully exposed stranger said as he stopped.

The darkness of a moonless night helped hide what was not covered, and Ceese helped everyone understand who stood before them.

"Joachim," she breathed out.

Geoffrey grimaced at the flayed skin, the deep scratches on the werewolf's back. "He's been attacked by some animal."

Joachim growled low when Geoffrey made an effort to assist him with his burden.

"He doesn't want help," Ceese said.

"Will he allow me to raise his trousers then? I believe my belt will work to secure them."

Ceese nodded, and Geoffrey worked quickly to remedy the young man's state of undress.

At some point during the fall, Brendan lost consciousness; Penny wanted to know. Ceese answered for Joachim. "He says he put him to sleep so he wouldn't fight the landing."

"We're secure here," Geoffrey said of Joachim's pants, and he straightened to stand.

Penny turned to Ceese. "Can you tell him to follow us inside then?"

Cassie walked beside Penny as they went. "Is this the werewolf from your vision?" Penny asked.

Cyn No More

"Oddly enough," Cassie replied. "I don't get the feeling that it is."

"Let's hope the one from your vision isn't the one that mauled Joachim's back, then—if a werewolf is at fault, that is."

* * *

Rodney and Kyle skidded on their feet around the corner just as the others entered from outside. "I'm sorry, Ceese," Rodney sputtered, out of breath. "I tried to stop him from jumping—" his eyes fell on the procession as it passed. "Who is he, and why is he carrying Brendan?"

"Joachim," Ceese said. "He saved Brother."

"Joachim? *The* Joachim?"

"Yes," Ceese nodded, followed after the others. Rodney astutely studied the werewolf's lean muscular build, his dark hair—his mutilated back.

"Brendan's room is this way," Penny said, directing the rescuer along.

Kyle came to stand behind Rodney. "Looks like her old boyfriend came to the rescue."

"Only because you're an idiot. I could've saved Brendan if you hadn't busted out onto the roof, yelling as though no one could hear you."

"What difference does it make now? He's alive, isn't he?"

191

Sue Dent

The difference, Rodney thought, is that he was supposed to save Brendan, not Joachim.

Chapter 31

JOACHIM PLACED BRENDAN ON the bed but did not step away. Instead, he moved his hands over the big man's lower abdomen.

"What's he doing?" Penny asked Ceese, certain that she knew.

"He's taking on the bruises, healing Brother in the same manner that Brother took Zade's scratches from me."

Joachim moved to the ankle next. Spent a little time there, then sank to a knee, weakened by his new injuries and his healing Brendan.

"Will he allow me to help him now?" Geoffrey asked.

Joachim answered for himself, perfectly imitating the butler. "Yes, I will allow it, especially since you are so eager to help."

Ceese followed the two out of the room.

"Do you think it's safe for her to be alone with Joachim?" Cassie questioned.

"I don't think she'd go if she didn't feel she could trust him."

Sue Dent

Penny turned to Marissa. "You can have your job back if you want it."

"Yes, ma'am."

"Just let me know when he wakes up. We'll be in the parlor trying to make sense of all of this."

* * *

Michelle held the torn-off tabloid cover up to compare one to the other. She knew right away that the two castles, the one in the picture and the one the taxi approached, were the same.

"That's it there," she said, pointed it out to the driver. He pulled into the drive. "I'll just need to go get someone to help me with my friend."

She made her way up the front walk and knocked.

After a long moment, Geoffrey answered.

She waved, smiled, and said, "remember me?"

Not in the mood to humor her, he said, "You shouldn't be here. It's not safe."

"Yeah, that's what the delivery driver said too. You know, the one who saw something out here that made him quit his job."

"Perhaps you should have listened to him then. You should leave."

Cyn No More

She stopped the closing door with her foot. "You might want to come and have a look inside the taxi first."

* * *

Those in the parlor gawked at Geoffrey half dragging Josh along.

"Whoa!" Kyle yelped, standing from his seat at Richard's armoire computer. "He's ripped!"

"He had this on him," said the woman who followed Geoffrey in, showed the rubber tourniquet. Geoffrey made a rushed introduction. "This is Michelle. She escorted Master Josh home."

"You found that on him?" Rodney said as he helped Geoffrey move Josh over to a couch where they sat him down.

"Yeah. It fell off during the taxi ride."

Severely nodding; drifting in and out of awareness, Josh said, "—speedball. . . I tol' Henderson I don't do speedballs," he slurred.

"Geoffrey," Penny said, tense. "Perhaps you should see Michelle out now?"

"Yes, of course."

"I do appreciate you bringing our friend home, dear, but—" Before Penny could finish her sentence, Rodney called for help holding a convulsing Josh. Geoffrey rushed over.

Rodney turned to Kyle. "Okay, pharmacy-boy. Assuming a speedball is the culprit, what are we dealing with?"

"Well, a speedball's a mix of cocaine and heroin but, the stimulant effects of cocaine wear off way faster than the depressant effects of heroin. Therefore, there's nothing to counter its effects, which could lead to fatal respiratory depression."

"Meaning?" Rodney prodded at Kyle dragging things out.

"He can't breathe."

Geoffrey helped as Rodney prepped Josh for mouth to mouth; pinched his nose closed and moved to clear the airway.

"Oh look," Kyle chirped, "fangs. He's a vampire again."

Rodney jumped up and back. "Is that even possible? Can a person just be a vampire again?"

Josh's convulsions calmed. His pupils became less constricted, and he sat up, the effects of the drugs subdued by the vampire.

Still sporting fangs, Josh said, "dude, that was some trip." His eyes fell on Michelle. "Whoa, maybe I'm still tripping. I remember her."

"That's Michelle," Geoffrey told him. "She helped bring you back here."

Cyn No More

Josh put a hand to his mouth, felt his fangs. "Henderson said he wasn't gonna curse me again. Said I was more trouble to him as a vampire."

"I don't think he cursed you," Penny offered. "Sometimes, the selfless-act isn't enough to effect a full recovery."

"Are there no set rules?" Rodney said, frustrated.

Kyle's nerves got the best of him. "Shouldn't you be out hunting or something?"

"Oh, yeah. Right." But Josh stopped short of leaving and patted himself down. "Where's my jacket? Henderson made me take it off—to shoot-up. Rodney, I gotta have my jacket."

"That stupid jacket," Kyle muttered. "We almost got caught trying to bust your vampire butt out of the hospital because of that jacket."

Rodney understood what it meant to Josh, though; losing his shield against his stepfather's beatings when he was old enough to fight back but wouldn't.

"I'll go into town tomorrow and look for it. I promise."

"Yeah. Okay," Josh nodded, his dreads following the motion of his head. "Thanks."

No sooner did he leave than Marissa showed up, wringing her hands and looking quite out of sorts.

Could it be more bad news about Brendan? Penny wondered. "Please tell me you've only come to report that he's awake."

Marissa nodded. "And he wants to see Master Rodney."

"Me," Rodney howled. "Why would he want to see me? He hates me. The last time I was in the same room with him, he nearly choked me to death."

"Did he say what he wanted with Rodney?" Penny asked.

"Yes, ma'am," she said, but the young servant seemed reluctant to say more.

"Well, let's have it, then."

"He wants Master Rodney to come to his room to shoot him because he believes that killing one's self is a sin."

* * *

Josh wandered around the grounds outside and followed the scent of something big, something other than an animal. In that same instant, everything went dark. All he could recall afterward was lying next to Peter Drummond, a look of horror frozen on the goatherder's ghastly, white face and a set of bite-marks on his thick neck.

Chapter 32

"HAVE YOU EVER DEALT with someone wanting to commit suicide," Cassie asked. "Do you even know what to say?"

Rodney prepared to stuff earbuds into his ears. "Weren't you listening?" he said to Cassie. "He wants me to kill him. That's not suicide. That's homicide which I'm technically against—unless provoked, of course, and that would be self-defense." To her growing look of concern as he pressed the earbuds in, he added, "anyway, I got this." He hit play on his phone's screen and began to whisper-sing The Frays *How to Save a Life.* "Step one, you say we need to talk. He walks, you say sit down it's just a talk . . ." Cassie shook her head back and forth as he left room for the hall.

Less than five minutes later, Rodney returned, his hands in the air, his earbud's dangling, and Brendan's shotgun pointed at his back.

Penny targeted Brendan with harsh words. "Suicide's a sin but killing, someone else isn't?" She changed her tone at his unstable look. "I'm sure we can talk about this."

Sue Dent

Rodney shakily responded. "Telling him that doesn't work. Just puts you at the business end of his shotgun."

Eyes fixed on Penny; Brendan growled. "What sort of sorcery have ye performed that has me up and about again, *seer*?"

Now was not the time to take him to task for calling her what she would rather not be called. "None. I swear it. If you have to place blame, then take it up with Joachim. He arrived just in time to catch you. He took on your wounds. He's resting now, Brendan."

Michelle gasped at hearing the name. "It is you."

Brendan stared in return, not daring to believe. "Ye must be a ghost," he said, his voice breaking with emotion. "Ye have to be. I buried ye so many years ago."

Her voice wavered in reply. "If I'm a ghost, then you are too—and have been for far too long."

Brendan side-eyed Penny. "This is yer doing. Ye're making me see things, and I told ye I nae need yer help in this matter."

"I'm not doing anything, Brendan. Whoever you think you see, is real. She's real."

"I see her," Rodney confirmed, itching to get away from the end of Brendan's shotgun.

"I see her, too," Cassie replied.

Cyn No More

"You'd have to be blind not to see her," Kyle interjected.

"It's me, Bren," Michelle said. "It's Gwen." He inhaled sharply, her words piercing his very heart. "And I swear, I will die where I stand if I have to wait one more second to feel your touch again."

Brendan shoved his gun into its holster, his rush over to his beloved bested only by Rodney's hurry to get out of the big man's way. A full embrace followed, and, with his head in her hair, he whispered in her ear, "I nae even care how ye're here."

"It was Zade," she obliged. "But I will not let him ruin this moment by talking about that monster."

Brendan put his hand to her face. "Nor will I ask you to." Kyle's get-a-room groan followed them out of the parlor.

The others in the room left shortly afterward, but Penny caught Cassie by an arm before she could go. "I need to show you something."

Penny closed the two parlor doors and led Cassie over to a bookcase behind Richard's desk, opened it, and led Cassie down to the room where she kept her diaries.

Cassie stared in awe at the number of shelved and stacked books. "These are all yours?"

"Yes," Penny said, "almost a century's worth of memories. I wanted you to see something specific, though." She picked out the diary with the bookmark and the note in it. "I came down here this morning to look in the diary where I wrote about the night Richard, and I first met. This is how I found it, the bookmark already in it, and this note tucked inside." Penny handed it over.

He's all mine now, it read.

"You didn't write this?"

"No, and that's Richard's handwriting."

Penny told Cassie all about the night before and what she missed after going to bed. She told her how Cyn used the *daoine maithe* to manipulate Richard and to possess him.

"I changed the combination shortly after I found the diary with those words written by Richard's hand. But you see how she can operate through him. Proves that he wasn't the one that attacked you but rather Cyn operating through Richard. Read the rest of the entry."

"I wouldn't feel comfortable," Cassie said, reluctant.

"It's all right. I need help figuring out why Cyn would waste her time coming down here and leaving that note."

Cassie took a minute to read, then looked up. "He sincerely hates the ocean, doesn't he?"

"To this day. Do you have any other opinions about what you read?"

Cyn No More

"Not necessarily an opinion. More like a question," and she scrunched her brow. "What would drive someone to go to a place they hate so much?"

Penny suddenly recalled something Meri told her the night before, and her expression changed to that of someone finishing a challenging puzzle. "Not what," she said, "who."

Cassie tried to keep up as Penny headed back to the parlor and over to Richard's armoire computer. She stood behind Penny as her grandmother googled the River Forth.

"That's it," Penny said, "the waters are brackish."

"I'm afraid I'm not understanding."

"Last evening, Meri said that Julia jumped in the River Forth to escape Cyn. Those were his exact words. She jumped in even though she couldn't swim to get away from Cyn. She knew something, and I suspect since we now know that Julia didn't die as Brendan thought, that she got that information to Richard that night."

Cassie's eyes grew wide. "The saltwater. It must weaken her scenting abilities."

"And significantly enough so that she couldn't find Richard," Penny added.

Chapter 33

"THAT HAS TO BE IT," Meri said, after coming into the parlor from hunting, and after listening to Cassie and Penny tell him what they decided must be the truth. "I never did understand why Julia jumped in the river to get away from Cyn when she couldn't swim. Never even put much thought into it. Congratulations on a job well done. But Richard hates the sea. I got him to go sailing with me a couple of times. He spent the entire trip glued to the deck, sick."

"I guess it all depends on what he hates more," Penny said, "the sea or Cyn."

On the heel of her sentence, the front door burst open, and Josh rushed in carrying a dead Peter Drummond across his arms.

"Meri," he said, seeing his mentor. "I killed him. I'm sorry. I thought I was stronger."

Penny responded to Meri's confused look. After all, Josh wasn't a vampire the last time he saw him. "It seems that the cure didn't hold."

"You fed on the goat herder?" Cassie said to Josh in disbelief.

Cyn No More

"Nonsense," Meri said, going over to him. "Show me your teeth." Josh did. "Your fangs," Meri said, "show me your fangs."

Josh did a quick half-way transformation, and Meri measured the distance with a thumb and a forefinger. He found the bite marks on Drummond's neck and held his spread fingers up to them.

"See," he said, showing what he found. "The distance is too close to be you. Someone else fed on him."

"And I smell jasmine," Penny remarked with an edge to her words.

"Why did you think it was you?" Meri asked Josh.

"I scented him. After that, I don't remember anything except waking up next to him."

"You should give yourself more credit," Meri said, patting him on the shoulder. "I do."

"Meri," Penny said cautiously. "We can't have Cyn going around all willy-nilly feeding off innocents. It will undoubtedly draw unwanted attention if anyone finds out."

"I'm fairly certain this kill wasn't willy-nilly, as you say, but rather intentional. Human blood will serve Cyn better than blood from another source."

"What if someone else had found Peter?"

"That's not her concern. She'll be gone as soon as she has Richard."

Cassie had a question. "Why put Josh near the body?"

Penny offered her opinion. "I suspect that was Henderson taking advantage of the situation. Another way to get back at Josh."

Meri turned to Josh. "Let's go give the goat-herder a proper burial."

"Meri," Penny said. "Have you seen Richard tonight?"

"I have. He fed and went to his coffin."

"Does he think he's any safer there?"

"I don't think he feels safe anywhere with Cyn around. Perhaps he'll respond favorably to being shipped out to sea. I'll come back once Josh, and I finish. We can work on a plan."

* * *

Penny entered the room where Ceese sat with Joachim. "How is he?"

"He's still resting."

"Those scratches are looking better, but do you know what happened to him?"

"I think he tried to rejoin the pack."

"It doesn't appear to have gone well for him."

Cyn No More

"He's different. To them, different is weak."

"I'm confused. Wasn't Joachim with this same pack before. His being different didn't seem to matter then."

"That's because Tobias stood up to the others for him."

"The Tobias that ended up on our doorstep courtesy of Zade?"

Ceese nodded confirmation.

A rapping at the door distracted, and Meri, returning from burying Drummond, entered. "I just saw the butler in the hall, Cee Cee. He told me that your little werewolf friend arrived and saved Brendan. Is he awake? I want to thank him."

Moving closer and catching sight of the werewolf's profile and then his full face, Meri's eyes grew wide, and he gasped as he sank into a chair next to the bed.

"Joachim," came his breathless whisper. "Brother. How can it be?" It had been so long ago since he had seen him that not even the name caused him to think that this Joachim was his brother. Meri reached out a hand to touch him only to have its wrist grabbed in an instant.

Joachim began speaking in their father's voice, reciting a memory, it seemed. "Take him away before he hurts the baby. Jerimiah is quite colicky and loud when he cries out. I fear Joachim's reaction to the noise. Take your brother somewhere safe; somewhere

Sue Dent

he can stay. He's old enough to be on his own now anyway."

"Yes," Meri said gently to Joachim. "Father did say that, and I did as he asked, didn't I? I helped you build a small cabin and, I visited you every day, brought you food until you could manage on your own. Then, one day—I came, but you weren't there. Two days, three days. You were as old as you are now, brother. What happened? Where did you go?"

"Zade found me and took me," Joachim said, in his real voice, a soft voice that Meri always considered quite melodic.

But the information confused Meri. "Why would he take you? He wanted Father. He wanted me. He wanted us to stop spreading the gosp—" Meri grabbed at his temple with his free hand, reworded. "Wanted us to stop teaching. You were no threat to him."

"Destroy the roots and the tree will die."

"This is what he told you?"

Joachim let the hand holding Meri's wrist fall. "So tired," he said, his eyes closing. "Must rest."

"Uncle," Ceese whispered at some horrible memory. "Tobias was right." Meri turned to see tears streaming. "It was my fault that Zade killed Joachim that day. Zade threatened to kill him many times and only stopped when Joachim cried 'uncle.' I thought he was asking Zade for mercy. But the very last time

208

Cyn No More

Joachim said 'uncle'—Zade took him anyway. He told him that it no longer mattered, that he had me now, and didn't need him anymore. Tobias blamed me, and now I understand why."

Meri stood and pulled her to him. "Cee Cee, you saved Joachim. Don't ever forget that. Zade is gone, in part because of you, and Joachim is back now, also because of you. I, for one, thank you because I have my brother back."

Penny stared in utter shock. "What on earth is wrong with him, Meri? You both act as though you don't see it."

"He's just—different, that's all," Meri tried.

"Yes. That's what Ceese said. But I'm not buying it. Your father put him out because he feared he might hurt a baby for making too much noise. Meri! That's not different. That's insane."

"He doesn't react well to loud noises. He's more of a threat to himself than anyone else. You saw. He saved Brendan tonight. Took on his injuries even after being mauled himself. Does that sound like someone who's a danger to others?"

"Sounds like you're trying to convince yourself as well as me."

"He won't be your concern. Cee Cee and I," he said, "we'll look after him. You won't have to worry. Right, Cee Cee."

Ceese's nod conveyed only a little of the confidence she hoped to portray.

* * *

Penny told Cassie to wait in the parlor for their planning session to begin. Thirty minutes later, neither Penny nor Meri had shown up. Curiosity got the best of her. Cassie strolled over to the bookcase, felt around for the catch, and pushed. At the bottom of the stairs, she keyed-in the code that Penny entered earlier and went inside. She wanted to know more about her mother and thought perhaps she could find more in the diaries. There were indeed enough of them. She picked one of the older books up but jumped at a noise behind her. She turned to see Penny.

"What are you doing here?" Penny said with a look of alarm and disappointment.

"I just—well, I thought—" What could she say? She was in a room filled with her grandmother's most private thoughts without permission. She handed over the diary she held. "I'm sorry. I just thought I might learn something more about my mother."

"I've told you everything I know," Penny said sternly, while simultaneously reeling in her anger just a bit.

"Just hard to accept, I guess, that I know so little."

"Hard to accept for me as well, as your great-grandmother kept her from me."

Cyn No More

Cassie nodded. "You can change the code," she said of the lock, "but you won't need to. I won't come down here again unless you bring me."

Chapter 34

ACTING MUCH LIKE HONEYMOONERS, Brendan and Gwen got up late the next morning and decided, after breakfast, to take their catching up and filling-in-of-blanks, outside on a stroll.

"Ye go by Michelle now," Brendan said, "but I cannae get used to calling ye anything other than Gwen."

"And you'd better not. I only went to my middle name because Gwen reminded me too much of you."

They abandoned the smooth walkway for the lawn and then moved into the forest.

"Ye say Zade came to ye on the eve of yer death." She nodded. "Promised to return ye're youth and to give ye immortality and some additional perks if ye helped draw me to him."

"I didn't think you could survive without me, Bren. His changing me to give me the time to find you—it was a compelling offer."

He raised his brows. "Aye, a compelling offer, indeed. Ye trade me in for immortality."

Cyn No More

Her reaction was immediate. "What? You think for one second that I planned on turning you over to him—"

Brendan laughed at her response to his subtle hints at her possible traitorous behavior. "Aye, there's much to be said of a woman who will turn their beloved over to his biggest enemy so that they can live forever."

She shoved at him hard, and he laughed louder, taking her to the ground, both landing softly on the carpeted-with-leaves forest floor and then rolling onto their sides to face each other.

"But what did Zade want with me anyway? Had he not done enough already?"

"You frightened him, Bren. You bested him in battle, and no one had ever done that. Certainly no mortal."

"Aye, but I had two arms at the time. I'm not the man that bested him anymore."

"Don't kid yourself. You're a warrior, Bren. You always have been. You just have to learn to do it with one arm and without werewolf prowess. But—" she added, poked at his chin. "You do need to grow your beard back."

He grinned. "Aye, ye miss it, do ye?"

"Aye, that I do!" she said, affectionately mocking him.

She rolled him onto his back, but before she could hit her intended target with her lips, he winced in pain, lifted his head.

With his one arm, he reached around, sat up, and gawked at what he found.

"Is that the knife," Gwen said, "the one you said you killed Zade with?"

"Aye, it is," Brendan said, moved to stand. "But I nae could find it when I went looking for it that night, the night we killed him."

Gwen stood up next to him. "Maybe you just missed it.

"Even if I did, it should nae be here." He looked warily around. "This is too far away from where it happened. Aye, someone put it here for us to find, and since I'm not sure who that someone might be, I say we should head back to the castle."

* * *

Rodney, with Kyle in tow, found Geoffrey in the kitchen. "We need a ride into town to try to find Josh's jacket. Maybe that chauffeur guy can take us. You know, the one you spoke with on that archaic phone that day."

A chagrinned smile played on Geoffrey's lips. "I'm sorry, but there is no chauffeur guy."

"Oh. Did he quit?"

Cyn No More

"Not exactly."

Rodney's face showed shock. "Dude, you lied to me?"

Kyle guffawed behind him. "Ha! He played you."

"I apologize," Geoffrey said, "I felt it was necessary to get your attention. But if you can give me a few minutes, I can take you to town myself. You can wait for me at the car. I'll only be a second."

"Sure," Rodney said, turned to see Ceese

"I want to go with you," she said. "I want to help."

"Don't you want to sit with your uh—your werewolf friend?"

Kyle, not one to miss an opportunity to irritate, coughed the word 'boyfriend' at Rodney's back.

Ceese eyed Kyle directly. "He's not that. He's not my boyfriend. He's my uncle."

A door opened at the end of the hall. Geoffrey called out. "Master Rodney, I'm able to take you now."

Rodney and Ceese slid into the back. Geoffrey found Rodney in the rearview mirror. "Do I need to wait for Master Kyle?"

Sitting particularly close to Ceese, Rodney replied, "no. He's staying here."

Chapter 35

GEOFFREY SEEMED TO KNOW exactly where to drive and even where to park. He pointed at a pub across the street. "Ms. Michelle works there. She bought Master Josh home after her shift. There's a good chance the jacket might be around here. Shall I assist in the search?"

"We got this," Rodney said, stepped out of the car after Ceese. "How hard could it be?"

The pair started in the alley behind the pub. "Should we split up?" Ceese asked.

"I think we work better as a team. I mean—don't you?" He said this as though he needed her assurance.

"Yes," she said, agreeing.

"And hey," Rodney added, pulled out his phone, "Josh said his cell was in his jacket, so—," he said, dialing Josh's number, "—if the battery isn't dead—"

Both faces brightened upon hearing the faint Guns 'N Roses ringtone. They ran to track it down; around a corner, down another alley. They stopped in their tracks at the sight of five street punks. The one that wore Josh's jacket turned to face them when the ringtone abruptly stopped.

Cyn No More

"You calling me, mate?" he said

Rodney put his phone away. "I know it sounds weird, but I was calling the jacket. It belongs to my friend. He lost it in the alley last night."

"Is that right?" the thug said, moving toward them.

"Yeah."

"Well, I found it, so that makes it mine now." The remaining four punks moved in, surrounding them.

"Look, It isn't worth anything, so why don't you just give it back, and we'll be on our way. You want a reward? I can get you a reward."

The apparent leader removed the jacket and fake-handed it over before tossing it to the ground behind him. "I'd rather fight you for it."

"I'm not gonna fight you ov—"

A colossal jab to his mid-section took Rodney's breath and doubled him over. He looked back and up at Ceese and gasped, ever the survivalist. "Are they here—the fey? Are the fey, here?"

"The *daoine maithe*?" Ceese asked as she looked around. "Yes, they're here. Quite a few, in fact."

The thug laughed, pulled Rodney upright. "Fairies, eh? You think I don't know what you're talking about? You think a bunch of fairies are gonna save you?" He glanced at the others around him. "Did you hear that?"

"Fairies," they all guffawed.

Sue Dent

The leader pulled back his arm and grinned. "I'd say that if the fairies are gonna save you, they better hurry."

The swing went wild, the arm indecently twisting the wrong way seemingly on its own accord. Rodney lunged forward and grabbed the jacket from the ground and Ceese by the hand and ran.

Ceese helped him along, but he was still too out of breath from the fist-slam to the gut to move very fast. To top it off, somewhere along the way, they made a wrong turn, and before they knew it, they were facing the same street punks, a few limping, some holding their side.

The leader went over to Rodney, reached out an arm. "Let's have it. Give me that jacket."

"Keep it," a voice said. Geoffrey appeared from around a corner.

"Go away, old man," the leader groaned, "and we'll promise not to hurt you."

"I'm not going anywhere without my friends and that jacket."

The leader held his hands out to his side. "There's five of us and only one of you."

"I dare say," Geoffrey said, "As I see it, there's one of me and only five of you."

Cyn No More

The fight was short-lived. Two punks fell fast. The other three opted to scatter, dragging their further-injured friends in retreat.

Rodney looked at Geoffrey from the wall where he leaned; knees bent slightly. "Please tell me you know the way out of here, G-man. I don't think I can run much further."

"Come along," the butler answered.

* * *

It was late afternoon by the time they arrived back at the castle. Stepping out of the car with Ceese, Rodney awkwardly leaned down to brush her lips with a kiss. He'd been planning it the entire ride back; was going to wait for Geoffrey to turn away, was going to make it quick so the butler couldn't see.

"Thanks for coming along. I'm glad you didn't get hurt."

"I'm sorry you did," she said, equally awkward but smiling. "I think I'll go check on my uncle now."

Rodney reached in and took the bomber jacket from the back seat before turning to Geoffrey. "Can you come with me to the basement? I don't like to go down there by myself, but I want to get this to Josh."

"Certainly," and then as they walked, "you fancy her."

"You weren't supposed to see that."

Sue Dent

"There's no shame in it."

"I was just thanking her."

"Of course."

"You're very nosy for a butler." Moving down the basement steps, Rodney added, "and you didn't have to take me to the ER. I told you I was fine."

"A&D," Geoffrey corrected. "And better safe than sorry."

"Really. You're gonna give me a foreign language lesson."

"English is hardly a foreign language."

"It is the way you speak it."

They abandoned the steps for the basement floor. Rodney moved to stand in front of Josh's coffin, took the cell from an inside pocket of the jacket. It would need charging. Cracking the lid just far enough, he began to shove the coat inside.

Without his help, the coffin lid flew open, drawing a surprised "Jeez," from Rodney. "I thought vampires were deep sleepers," he said as Josh sat up. "You nearly gave me a heart attack."

"You found it," Josh said, clutching the jacket.

"I said I would, didn't I? I just wanted it to be here when you woke up. Now go back to sleep."

"I—I can't. I'm all keyed up now!"

Cyn No More

"Well, get unkeyed up?"

Josh eyed Geoffrey and, in a low voice, said, "Can't you just stay with me until I fall asleep?"

"In the coffin?"

"Yeah, you know—just until I fall asleep." Josh seemed to be tailoring his words for the butler who did his best to pretend, for their comfort, that he wasn't paying attention.

"Dude, you're a vampire. I can't risk that."

"I won't bite you—"

Geoffrey tried to be subtle. "If that's your only concern, Master Rodney, you could wear my cross," and he removed it for Rodney to take.

"Just so you know," Rodney said, putting it on, "it's not what it looks like."

"It looks like a friend helping a friend," Geoffrey replied to Rodney crawling in. "Shall I knock you up later?" Rodney's eyes bugged. "Which, translated, means wake you," Geoffrey clarified. "Shall I wake you later."

"Oh, yeah. Right. No, I'm good. As soon as he's snoring, I'm out of here."

Rodney settled in behind Josh on his side, his front to Josh's back. "Shall I lower the lid," Geoffrey asked.

A simultaneous 'yes' and 'no' rang out.

"Dude," Rodney said. "I'm not a vampire. I need to breathe."

Geoffrey propped the lid at an angle. "How's that?"

"Works for me," Rodney replied, "and Josh doesn't get a say if he wants me to hang around."

Josh remained silent.

Chapter 36

"AYE, SO WHAT'S THIS ABOUT a planning session?" Brendan asked shortly after dinner as he walked into the parlor with Gwen.

Penny moved from behind Richard's desk. "Well, Cassie and I agree that we need to do something to protect Richard from Cyn."

"Yes," Cassie said.

Brendan stood stubbornly still and quiet.

"I know you're still upset over what happened in Cassie's bedroom," Penny said to Brendan's defiant look, "but that wasn't Richard. Cyn can work through him, and she did that night. Even at that, Richard was able to protect you by holding back punches as best he could and directing them where they would do the least amount of damage. Dr. Laguard confirmed this."

"So ye think I should thank him?"

His look was such that Penny welcomed the distraction of Ceese walking in with Joachim. She sighed with relief that Joachim wore clothes and looked quite dapper with his near blue-black hair, the one feature that set him apart from the other Porter men that she had met. But how would Brendan take to seeing him, knowing that he foiled his suicide plans?

"Brother," Ceese gasped, raced toward Brendan. It was the first time she had seen him since he jumped. "You're all right."

Brendan glanced at Joachim over her shoulder as he accommodated her hug. "Aye, it seems ye're friend caught me when I—slipped."

And so now it was an accident, Penny thought as she listened.

Brendan had said 'friend.' Ceese corrected him. "Uncle. Father says Joachim is our uncle."

Brendan faced the werewolf. "Well, uncle, the last time I saw ye was when I sent ye after Ceese when she was six years old. I would thank ye for returning her safely, but she showed up on the porch wrapped in Richard's coat, and ye were nowhere around."

"Zade was onto me. I had to run to protect her."

"Well, then I thank ye for that."

Ceese leaned over to whisper into Brendan's ear, at the same time pointing to the woman beside him.

Brendan smiled. "Aye, ye missed her arrival last night. This is Gwen. Gwendolyn Michelle McCarthy Porter be her full name." As Ceese's eyes widened, he added with a wink, "My wife and your aunt. She's a

Cyn No More

victim of Zade's as well. She took advantage of her immortality and restored youth to find me."

"You can call me Michelle. Everybody else does."

"Is that what he calls you?" Ceese said of Brendan.

"He calls me Gwen."

"Then that's what I'll call you."

Penny watched Cassie's face drop. Ceese opened up so quickly to the young woman. "I'm sure it's because of their shared connection with Zade," Penny consoled in a whisper just loud enough for Cassie to hear. Penny then turned her attention back to Brendan. "So, can we count on your help then."

"My help?"

"Yes, your help."

Brendan's look suddenly turned cold. "Ye can count me out. Cyn can take him for all I care."

His harsh words brought Joachim over next to him. "Is the Mill Creek bridge that far from your memory that you can't recall what happened there? The ice-cold, rushing water. Little Dalia crying out."

"He didn't want to help," Brendan answered. "He never wanted to help, especially if it was my idea."

"Yet, he did and nearly drowned by your hand. If I hadn't saved him that day, he'd be dead now. And do you know why he helped you, nephew?" A stiff Brendan did not respond. Joachim switched to Father's

225

voice and added in Scottish Gaelic, "*tha fuil nas tighe na uisge.* Blood is thicker than water."

"Enough," Brendan snapped, affected by the words. And then to Penny, "yes. I'll help."

Chapter 37

RODNEY AWOKE WITH A START, still in the coffin with Josh. He looked at his watch. *Six-thirty!* He had fallen asleep. He scurried to climb out. Josh stirred and climbed out as well, slipping into his bomber jacket.

They both heard it at the same time, a moaning sound coming from Meri's coffin. Josh rushed to look in on his friend.

"Help me out," Meri groaned, the front of his shirt soaked with blood.

* * *

A ruckus in the hall took the attention of those in the parlor; The clamoring of voices, the shuffling about of feet. They ran out to investigate, passing Kyle at the door.

"Fine," Kyle said to their backs. "I won't tell you what I learned."

Josh and Rodney, with Meri between them, moved quickly down the hall. "We found him like this in his coffin," Rodney said.

They eased him down onto a couch. Meri, his breaths deep, said, "Cyn's responsible."

Sue Dent

"Again, Meri," Penny gasped. Geoffrey, who had seen the group in the hall, returned with supplies and quickly dressed the wound.

"I can fix you," Joachim said.

"You can't fix me, brother. Cyn has the power to say when I live and die, and she has spoken."

"That's ridiculous, Meri," Penny said.

"Is it?" Meri countered. "You know she has my soul; I've told you this, and I've shown you. Now it seems she's tired of my interfering with her efforts to keep Richard away from her. With this wound, I will not make it through the night. I'm dying, and when I do, I'll go straight to hell. And, for the record, she's already taken Richard."

"Begging your pardon," Geoffrey said, "but I checked on m'lord earlier. He's still resting in his coffin."

"She took him when she did this to me. She'll come back for his body when it's more convenient."

Penny struggled with his words. Something about them didn't ring true. "After everything that you've done to keep Cyn from Richard—you're just going to sit by and let her take him now?"

He reacted fiercely. "Over my dead body."

Meri asked for his Bible Box. Brendan retrieved it and sat it on the table in front of him.

Cyn No More

"How are ye not affected?" Brendan asked of Meri opening the box and taking his old Gaelic Bible out to turn its pages.

"Cyn has taken the vampire away so I can die."

"That was thoughtful of her," Cassie remarked.

Meri sighed optimistically, stared at two blank pages. "Ah, here it is."

"Aye, here what is? There's nothing there."

"On these pages is a tome of sorts designed to transport the seventh son of a seventh son into the realm of the *doine mathe*."

"Tome?" Cassie said, staring at the same 'nothing' that Brendan just mentioned. "There are no words."

"Sure, there are," Meri assured her, but only a seventh son can see them. And for the tome to work, the words have to be read by another seventh son."

"And why would you want to be transported there, brother?" Joachim asked.

For the first time in a long time, Meri's eyes held tears. "To escape damnation and to be with my Julia."

That got Brendan's attention. "Mother? She's dead. I buried her."

Rodney rolled his eyes. "You buried your wife too, but there she is, standing right beside you. Can you bury me when I die?"

Sue Dent

"Wife?" Meri said, easily ignoring Rodney.

Brendan temporarily brushed past his confusion over mother being alive for a quick introduction. "Yes, this is Gwen. She arrived yesterday—and is alive courtesy of Zade. Most likely the only good thing he ever did, albeit unintentionally."

Meri acknowledged Gwen with a brief but warm smile. "I'll bet you would do anything for her."

"I would die for her."

"Then you know how I feel about Julia. And she didn't die that night. As I understand it now, Cyn took her. She used Julia to get to the *daoine maithe,* her family, and yours. She wanted the power they offered — the ability to achieve an ethereal form. Your mother is alive, a prisoner of Cyn's. Using this tome, I can be with her again. I can avoid this fate I've set for myself to save my children."

Brendan, slowly taking the words in, said, "aye, but nae one of us is a seventh son."

"Ceese is the seventh born," Meri said. "That should be good enough."

Ceese looked over his shoulder at the pages. "But I don't see anything, Father. The pages are blank."

Meri sank into despair. "I was certain it would work."

Cyn No More

Josh looked over Ceese's shoulder. "You can't see those words?"

All eyes turned to Josh. Meri's look turned hopeful. "You can?"

"Well, yeah," and he started to read.

"No, no, no, no," Meri said excitedly, waving his hands in front of him and grinning ear to ear. "Not yet, son. Not yet."

Chapter 38

RODNEY EYED JOSH AS though he were from outer space. "You're the seventh born boy of a seventh son? You only have five brothers."

Josh shrugged. "I don't know how many times my ol' man hooked up before he got with my mom."

Penny and Cassie both cringed at his vernacular.

Cassie then asked Meri, "can it work like that? Grandmother gave me some books. I've been reading up on different things. Doesn't it have to be a clean line on both sides—mother and father?"

"Just paternal," Meri said. "Biblical David had six sons from other wives in Hebron before Bathsheba gave birth to his seventh son, Solomon." Meri smiled up at Josh. "I knew you were special."

"Oh, he's special all right," Kyle cackled.

"But Meri," Penny asked before Kyle could take his words any further, "how does any of this help Richard?"

"Right." With no time to spare, Meri shared his idea for a plan, leaving nothing out and answered any final questions. "If that's it then," he said when they'd exhausted their questions, "then there's only one thing left to do."

Ceese sat down next to Father, held tight to his hand. "No tears, Cee Cee" he told her. "This isn't goodbye, right?" He looked up at Josh. "But it might be if we don't hurry."

Josh took the hint and began reading the words aloud.

* * *

"I suppose it's all up to us now," Penny said as Meri vanished before their eyes.

"Doesn't anybody wanna hear what I came in here to say?" Kyle asked as though nothing odd had just happened.

"Okay," Rodney said, "I'll bite. What did you come in here to say?"

"Those pellets you cut out of Ceese," he said to Cassie. "I looked at the combination again, especially the dosage level. It's basically a fertility cocktail." He turned to face Rodney. "She's so fertile right now, that even if you—"

Rodney shot him a look that shut him down. "Finish that sentence, and I will rip your lungs out."

"So touchy," Kyle said, raising both hands in surrender.

Sue Dent

Cassie turned to Penny. "Are you thinking what I'm thinking?"

Penny shook her head back and forth. "I wish I weren't."

Chapter 39

CRADLING RICHARD'S LIMP BODY in his arms, Geoffrey followed Penny, who led with a flashlight, along the empty dock on the Thames, and Cassie, who carried a bag of items Meri said they would need to aid in reuniting Richard with his body.

"Over here," Penny said, as she trudged through the briny muck left behind by receding brackish waters and into a shoreline cavern. She pointed out a flat-top bed of stone. "Just lay him there."

With Richard spread out on the slab, Cassie went to work, setting out the candles from the bag around Richard's body, placing them according to the pattern on the piece of paper she held; the sketch Meri provided before Josh read him into the realm of the *daoine maithe*. She then lit the candles and burned the piece of paper as instructed.

Afterward, she went to stand with Penny at the front of the cave to wait.

* * *

"How do you think this will look on my job resumé," Kyle said, stretched out on the ground behind a log with the others, waiting for the signal. "Assistant vampire/werewolf hunter. Should I list it under skills?"

With Brendan on the other side of Kyle, Rodney squinted at him. "Do you think you're far enough away from the one who threatened to tie you up so you couldn't follow us to be so snide?"

Kyle emulated a chokehold on his own neck, complete with gagging noises as a reminder of what Brendan had done to Rodney not that long ago.

Brendan's loud, 'shhh!' silenced them both.

*   *   *

"Julia," Meri gushed at seeing his beloved, at holding her when she fell into his arms only to push away seconds later. Raising distressed eyes to his, she said, "Cyn has Richard. I—I tried to stop her—we tried, but she said she would kill you if I tried anything else."

"She says a lot of things."

"But she's on her way now to get Richard's body."

"Perfect. There's a plan underway even as we speak. But I need your help." He looked around, "and I'll need the help of the *daoine maithe*. I know I'm not in a position to ask as I'm not one —"

A familiar tall-hatted, bearded fey moved up behind Meri. "It seems you are one of us now, and Richard certainly is. What do you need?"

236

Cyn No More

***

"I see them," Ceese said, "several of them out in front of the cave.

"Aye," Brendan nodded. "That be the signal. Uncle, ye know what to do."

Joachim stood and tucked the Bible box under an arm. Speaking in Meri's voice, he said, "I run till I reach the large cliff. I take the preaching bands stained with Richard's blood from the secret compartment in the Bible box and tie them around the rock." He shook the box to rattle the stone. "Then I throw the preaching bands over the edge of the cliff to put Cyn off Richard's true scent."

Kyle's mouth dropped open. "Let's hope Cyn's not anywhere around to hear all of that."

But Meri had instructed Brendan to get Joachim to repeat his mission before he was sent off to do it.

"Aye," Brendan said, in response to his Uncle's words. "We'll see ye back at the castle then."

The group behind the log stood to leave. Gwen posed a question to Brendan. "Are those two always so helpful?" she said of Kyle and Rodney.

"Aye," Brendan said, "welcome to my world."

***

237

Cassie stared mesmerized at the dancing orbs of light on the horizon. "They're beautiful, like the fireflies I used to see on my uncle and aunt's farm."

"I think it's time to move to the back of the cave," Penny said. "Meri was emphatic that we not watch."

* * *

They viewed the castle from behind thick bushes as Cyn, in ethereal form, exited and headed off into the forest and not toward the city."

"Aye, it looks as though she's taken the bait," Brendan said.

"It worked," Ceese said. "Joachim did it." Hearing the wolves in the distance; the barking, the howling, she uneasily added, "unless the pack found him first."

Brendan faced Ceese. "Why would the wolves be after him, sister?"

"He's weak. They know this. They will try to kill him."

"Of course," Brendan said, ran a frustrated hand through his hair. "But why would he volunteer to do such an important task that would take him straight through their territory? Aye, we could have sent anyone else."

"Bren," Gwen said gently, noting Ceese's somber look.

Cyn No More

Looking at Ceese, he took it down a notch. "I'm sorry, sister. I nae blame ye." He looked off toward the howls. "I'll go see if I can find him."

"Except that would be like a suicide mission," Rodney said. "Not that that's not your forté. But there's no way you can take on a pack of wolves."

"We nae even know if it's him they're after."

Gwen called to him when he turned to leave. He looked back over his shoulder. "*Bidh mi faiceallachto,*" he said before she could say more. "I'll be careful."

Chapter 40

FIRST, THE CAVE WENT DARK, the candles flickered out, and then a bright flash held steady for a matter of minutes, gradually dimming completely.

"How do we know when it's safe to turn around?" Cassie asked.

"Meri didn't say. He just said we'd know."

"Now would be a good time," Richard said, sitting up.

Penny switched on the flashlight. Geoffrey rushed over with the satchel he carried in with him. "You'll find two pouches of blood packed inside."

Richard clutched the butler by a forearm. "Geoffrey," he said, looking up, "could you help me to the back of the cave. I'm a bit unsteady."

"Of course, sir."

The three waited outside for Richard to finish feeding then, walked with Richard to the car.

"Was your father able to fill you in on everything?" Penny asked Richard, testing his state of mind. He hadn't said two words during the short walk back.

Cyn No More

"He did, and I understand that we need to get back to the castle."

Once in the car, Cassie, in the middle, Richard and Penny on either side, Penny said, "and there are a few new visitors at the castle that we probably need to tell you about."

* * *

Brendan found the pack and realized things were as feared; the wolves had found Joachim and, close on his heels, they chased him up the steep slope that ended in an even more precipitous drop. Forced to the edge, and with nowhere else to go, Joachim jumped.

Brendan stopped when the wolves turned on him. He had a decision to make; stand and die or run and die. The wolves, he knew, would show no mercy.

A distant howl grabbed their attention. Ears perked; they took off running. Brendan wasted no time making his way to the drop-off. He looked over the edge and spied Joachim hanging on to an exposed root.

He called out to his uncle and laid on the ground, reaching over the cliff.

"Take hold of my hand."

Joachim did, just as the root lost its hold in the earth. The quick transfer of weight sent Brendan sliding forward while someone grabbing hold of his ankles, brought him to a jerking halt. Someone grabbed hold of his ankles from behind.

241

Sue Dent

"Use both arms," Brendan heard.

"I would if I could."

Seconds after he spoke, he felt heat warm his body and felt stronger.

The voice repeated those three words. "Use both arms.

Brendan saw it then, out of the corner of his eye, and reached out with his new appendage to do just as the stranger asked. He held tightly to his Uncle as the one holding his ankles pulled. Safely on flat ground, Brendan rushed to stand and turned on a heel to identify the rescuer.

"Tobias?" he said, stunned. "Aye, the last time I saw ye was on the castle's doorstep flayed of yer skin courtesy of Zade." Brendan tested his left hand as he spoke, opening and closing it into a fist. "Is this permanent?"

Tobias nodded. "You help Tobias once," he said in werewolf-third-person. "Tobias not forget."

"Aye, helped ye remember how to change into your wolf-form," Brendan nodded. "It be barely a week ago."

"You help many. Tobias help you now, for himself. For the others."

"I feel stronger as well."

"Tobias give you more strength to hold Joachim."

242

Cyn No More

"Am I cursed?" Brendan asked with a look of concern.

"Does Brendan feel cursed?"

Brendan put his new hand on Joachim's shoulder. "Nae. I feel far from cursed. And I thank ye for helping me save my Uncle."

"Tobias thank you for helping him save his brother."

"Wolf-brother," Joachim said at Brendan's widening eyes. "Tobias is Joachim's wolf-brother. Blood brothers, too," and he showed a nasty scar on his wrist, reached over, and showed Tobias' wrist as well.

"Ye can protect him from those wolves then, those savages that ran him off the cliff?"

"Tobias sent them after Joachim, to bring him home. Tobias new pack leader. Tobias protect Joachim. Tobias always protect Joachim."

"So that howl, ye were calling them off, the wolves?" Tobias nodded. Brendan turned to Joachim. "Seems ye have a decision to make, then. Leave with Tobias or come back to the castle with me.

"I will come with you, Nephew. There is work left to do."

"Then pack comes too," Tobias said.

Sue Dent

Brendan flashed a worried look. "I'm not sure how I feel about that."

Joachim put an arm around his nephew's shoulders. "You won't even know they're with us."

Tobias signaled to the pack to follow. The wolves responded, howling vociferously. Brendan turned to his uncle.

"They'll quiet down," Joachim assured.

"I almost forgot to ask," Brendan said, "Did you get rid of the bands?"

"Of course. And left the box right where Meri told me to leave it."

* * *

Those at the castle heard the howls. Gwen seemed particularly anxious. Ceese spoke to her fears. "Brendan's all right. Those are good howls."

"Is there such a thing?" Kyle said.

* * *

Darrell, stiff from the long flight over, roused from his slumber. The plane would be landing shortly. He needed to stretch. He had booked the flight last minute with 'Daddy's Money' as Rodney called it and used his passport from the family trip to France a few years back.

Cassie meant the world to him. He'd do anything for her. He'd even taken a step down to attend

Cyn No More

Templeton instead of an Ivy League college to be closer to her, both physically and emotionally. But Rodney's recent lies completely derailed their relationship. Cassie stopped calling him and wouldn't return his texts. She completely shut him out. And right after opening up to him as well. She was letting him help her on her projects, trusting him.

He told her he felt Rodney was using her by playing on her sympathies, but he never pressured her to kick him out as a roommate, never said it was either him or Rodney.

The passengers were given the green light to gather their belongings. Darrell removed his carry-on from the overhead bin, snapped the telescoping handle out, and pulled the bag along behind him. *You've had it, Kincaid,* he thought to himself as he exited the plane into the terminal.

Chapter 41

"SO CEESE'S WEREWOLF FRIEND showed up out of thin air and saved Brendan from plummeting to his death?" Richard said.

Penny nodded. "Yes, and as it turns out, he's your uncle cursed by Zade so many years ago. But I must say, Joachim, worries me. There's something not right with him."

"If I may interject," Geoffrey said as he drove, "and I'm no expert on the matter. But I do have a cousin that suffers from autism spectrum disorder, a condition related to brain development that impacts how a person perceives or socializes with others. It could be that Master Joachim suffers from something similar. Social cues do seem to be a problem for him."

Cassie nodded. "That's an understatement."

"Regardless," Penny said of Geoffrey's comments, "he still worries me. And if Joachim being your uncle isn't far-fetched enough, there's more. You have a sister-in-law."

Richard leaned forward to look around Cassie at Penny, eyebrows raised. "Brendan? Married? Oh, do tell."

Cyn No More

"Gwen, also a victim of Zade's but not cursed, just affected, like Brendan or rather, like Brendan was before Zade's demise."

Geoffrey found Richard in the rear-view mirror. "You would know her as Michelle from the pub."

Richard seemed to take the news in stride. "That explains her Scottish accent then, I suppose."

"Wait," Cassie said. "You know her?"

"After Cyn used me to attack you, I found myself at the pub where Michelle—or rather Gwen works. My blood lust led me there. One thing led to another, and I ended up in the alley with her. But as you can see, I didn't curse her."

"You stopped yourself?"

"No. You stopped me." Cassie stared confused. "Michelle," he didn't bother to correct himself this time, "she pushed a strand of hair behind her ear the way you occasionally do. All I could see was your face, and I couldn't follow through. Next thing I knew, she wedged a foot behind mine and took me to the ground. She was off and running for the safety of the pub after that."

Penny stared out the window at the turn the conversation took, deciding to think more about what she just learned. Of all the patrons at the pub that night, Richard seemed to have targeted Gwen or was it vice-versa. Why did she get the feeling it wasn't a coincidence?

* * *

The trio of Brendan, Joachim, and Tobias slowed as they neared the castle. "I nae like it," Brendan said of the air-sucking brooding calmness all around.

"Bren," Gwen said, coming up to meet him, "It's too quiet."

Two arms embraced her. "Aye, much too quiet."

She pushed away, stared aghast at his new arm. "How?"

Rodney, Josh, Kyle, and Ceese, having followed her over, listened for the answer too.

"It's a very interesting story that we nae have time for at the moment." He pointed out the headlights coming down the lane. "The others are back."

The car pulled into the drive. Penny, Cassie, and Richard headed over.

"The plan worked," Penny said of Richard walking with them.

Cassie followed that comment up with one of her own, directed at Brendan. "Your arm," and then, another aimed at Tobias, "that's the werewolf from my vision."

"Aye, the one responsible for what you just noticed."

Cyn No More

Penny nodded. "Well, I guess we know why he's here, then."

The werewolf spoke for himself. "Tobias come for Joachim. Take Joachim home."

Rodney listened to Ceese's reaction to this comment. "He is home. This is his home."

Tobias growled low at the teen.

"Back off, Worf," Rodney said to the one he decided looked very much like the Klingon from 'Star Trek,' minus the ridged forehead.

"Dude," Kyle laughed, "he does look like Worf."

"Worf?" Josh said, clueless.

Kyle stared as though his friend was an alien from another planet. "Are you for real right now?"

Ignoring the banter, Richard acknowledged Gwen. "I apologize for my actions the other night. I was not myself."

Brendan stared suspiciously. "Aye, what's he talking about?"

"I tried to curse her," Richard said. Brendan drew an arm back. Richard took a defensive stance. "Not to worry. She has a temper to match yours. She took me down and escaped."

Richard moved on to talk to Joachim. "And I've been told that you're my uncle."

Sue Dent

"And you believe that?" Joachim replied.

Richard shot Penny a sideways glance then turned back to Joachim. "It's the truth, isn't it?"

Richard's own words from the past were thrown back at him in his own voice. "The truth is only as good as the one telling it."

Even though Richard recalled so little of his past, he suddenly remembered those words and their context; Brendan trying to warn him of Zade at Joachim's behest. Joachim dropped the impersonation.

"You called me a liar. You swore Brendan to silence."

"I'm sorry," Richard said. "Father told us not to speak of Mother's attack."

"Aye," Brendan piped up, "That he did. But ye dinna know what I knew. And ye would nae listen."

"That's because, at the time, you would believe anything anyone told you, especially if it was what you wanted to hear."

"That nae be the point. I'm ye brother. Ye own flesh and blood."

"A brother with bad judgment."

Brendan reached out with both arms, took Richard by his shirt collar, and drew him in close while Richard wrestled to hold the vampire back.

Chapter 42

PENNY WORKED QUICKLY TO DIFFUSE the situation. "Boys," she said. "Have you forgotten about Cyn? She is not going to react well to being tricked again. We need to come up with a plan."

"Yes," Joachim said, "perhaps Brendan can take a walk with his 'beloved' to clear his head." And he batted at the base of Brendan's skull hard enough to get his attention and hard enough to hopefully remind him of something that happened earlier when he and Gwen strolled the grounds.

All at once, Brendan released Richard, reached toward his holster that held its silver-bulleted, pistol-handled, sawed-off shotgun.

"Brother," Richard said, took a step back at the prospect of being shot. "I'm sure we can talk about this."

But instead of the shotgun, Brendan pulled something else from his holster; the *Akedah* knife.

Brendan had shoved it in his holster after finding it on the forest floor and after his head hit it when he rolled onto his back.

"Where did that come from? I thought you said it went with Zade," Richard said.

"I thought it did. But it showed up in a clearing not far from the castle this morning." Brendan turned to Joachim. "Did ye put it there, uncle? Ye must've since ye made that comment about Gwen and me."

"I didn't put it there," Joachim said.

"I wonder if it works with vampires the same way it works on werewolves." Cassie pondered.

"My sources say it does," Brendan replied.

Richard rubbed hard at the bridge of his nose. "By sources, do you mean the seller's description on eBay?" Brendan's eyes narrowed dangerously. "Don't get so worked up," Richard said to calm him. "I'm just trying to get my digs in while I can because if that knife doesn't work for vampires as it does for werewolves, none of us will be around to talk about it. Cyn doesn't show mercy to those who cross her."

"That's a good start for a plan, though," Cassie said.

"We certainly need to come up with something," Penny said with a sense of urgency.

"Well, I can't throw the knife the way I did to take Zade down," Richard said. "I can't touch it."

"Can't you give someone a quick lesson?" Cassie asked.

"It's not that simple."

"I know that's right," Kyle said. "Teaching darts isn't simple either."

Cyn No More

Rodney laughed out loud. "Not simple to teach darts? What's there to learn? You take a dart, and you throw it at a dartboard."

"If you play to win," Kyle retorted, "you have to learn things like how to hold the dart properly, balance, aiming, snapping the wrist and—" He stopped talking when he noticed all eyes were on him.

"Hand him the knife," Richard said, heading over to Kyle.

"Aye, ye have to be joking, Brother."

"Give him the knife or die at Cyn's hand."

"This is no dart," Kyle said, nervously handling the relic.

"It's close enough," Richard said, leading him onto the landscape lit lawn so Kyle could see better in the thick darkness. "It's just a big dart. See that tree—that leaf on the trunk. Can you hit it?"

Kyle tried and stuck it dead center. "You're right," Kyle laughed. "It is just a big dart."

"Now, let's try something further away. Over there, that leaf."

"Dude, that's too far away. You can't expect me to throw it that far *and* be accurate."

Richard stepped behind Kyle. "Aim," he said into his ear, at the same time putting a hand on Kyle's dart-throwing arm. "When I say now, throw it."

With Richard adding the power, the knife flew to its target.

"Bullseye!" Kyle erupted in a short-lived and irritating celebration dance.

Brendan glared and shook his head. "Ye couldn't use someone else?"

"It's all in the release and the wrist action, Brother. He's got it."

Chapter 43

GEOFFREY PARKED THE CAR, pulled the garage door closed, and secured the padlock. He stopped cold when he felt someone behind him.

"Why would Richard let his favorite pet wander around without a cross?" Cyn said very close to the butler's ear.

* * *

"She will have the element of surprise," Richard said to the group on the front lawn. "We'll need to be on guard."

A sudden and robust scent of Jasmine brought an immediate reaction from Kyle. "Surprise," he said with mock enthusiasm

Penny watched Richard closely. They couldn't do this without him, but his fear of Cyn overwhelmed him so much that she didn't know if he could get past it.

But Richard took charge and signaled the group to follow him around one side of the house where Cyn stood—holding Geoffrey captive.

"Look who I found," she said, speaking loud enough to be heard by the group who stopped a little over ten yards away and she licked seductively at his neck.

Sue Dent

"Where is his cross?" Richard whispered in a voice that reflected his concern.

"I have it," Rodney said, recalling. "He lent it to me. I never got it back to him."

Cyn buried her fangs in Geoffrey's neck. The butler writhed and cried out as she sampled his essence.

Richard agonized right along with him, knowing the pain firsthand. But more than that, he worried how much Geoffrey could take as a mortal.

"Stop it," Richard shouted when Cyn showed no sign of releasing Geoffrey. "You'll kill him."

Cyn pulled her fangs free. "That's the plan—a little snack before the main course. And you can only feel guilty about it because you're the reason I'm doing it. You could've cooperated, but you chose not to. Say goodbye to your little butler friend."

Cyn adjusted her aim then, bared her fangs, and opened wide.

* * *

A shadow figure separated itself from the darkness and swiftly moved up behind Cyn, who froze, mid-strike.

"That's a vampire," Josh revealed. "I can sense it."

"I agree," Richard replied. "I sense it too."

"Oh, snap," Rodney said, his eyes wide.

256

Cyn No More

Cassie turned toward him. "Oh, snap, what?"

"I think that's G-man's vampire dad."

Richard cut his eyes at Rodney. "Why would you think that? And how do you know about his vampire father? It's something he keeps to himself."

"Well, he told me how he'd been looking for him for some time without any luck. He seemed especially bummed about it, so I thought I'd try to find him."

"Geoffrey's been looking for years without any luck, and you find him in a matter of days?"

"Day. One day," Rodney corrected. "I found him in one day."

"How?"

"It's hard to hide in today's society when your initials are W-T-F-G, and you build luxury coffins for a living and advertise on the web."

"That's great," Kyle guffawed despite the circumstances, gestures a marquee with a hand, and looks as though reading it. "Way to freakin' go' luxury coffins."

"Anyway," Rodney continued. "I didn't know I found him. I just sent an email asking."

"Regardless," Richard said, "Geoffrey's safe for the moment, and we need to take advantage." He looked at the knife that Brendan held. "We need someone to

257

Sue Dent

donate their cursed blood. I'd do it, but I have to help Kyle throw the knife."

"You mean the way Meri did," Josh said.

Richard nodded. "Yes. But you must consider that there is a risk involved. I don't know how Father survived being stabbed by such a significant—uh—'relic,' but I suppose there was a chance that the act could have killed him."

Josh didn't hesitate with his answer. "I understand. I'll do it."

Brendan handed Kyle the knife since Richard could not directly touch it without being adversely affected.

"I'll guide Kyle's hand to avoid damaging any vital organs."

Josh stared at Kyle's devilish grin. "No, not Kyle. Rodney."

The knife switched hands. Brendan moved to stand behind Josh. "Just in case ye pass out," Brendan said. "I'll ease ye down."

As the point entered his body, Josh grimaced. The deeper it penetrated, the more his distress grew. After a few seconds, Richard eased Rodney's hand that held the knife, out, and Josh's face fell full-on slack, his body limp.

Cyn No More

"Aye," Brendan said to Rodney's distressed look and at the same time easing Josh to the ground, "he probably just needs to rest."

"Next challenge," Richard said, "We've got to get Cyn in the open."

"Joachim," Ceese said, "he's strong and fast."

"Yes," Joachim said, "Tobias can help too."

"None of this will work if Cyn sees them coming," Gwen offered.

"Aye," Brendan agreed, standing after lowering Josh. "We need a distraction."

"The pack," Joachim said. "Tobias can call the pack."

* * *

"I am fully prepared to die for my son," the vampire growled into Cyn's ear.

Geoffrey managed a weak, "no, Father."

"Listen to the boy," Cyn replied. "It doesn't have to be like this. I don't want him anyway. You turn me loose, and I'll turn him loose."

"You turn him loose, and I'll consider it."

The howls echoed too close for comfort, as the wolf-pack raced pell-mell toward them. Distracted as planned, Joachim and Tobias changed from into their human form and snatched Geoffrey and his father as they ran past Cyn.

A handful of wolves broke away and circled the vampire, preventing her from running, as they worked to move her into position.

* * *

"Now," Richard said into Kyle's ear, his arm on Kyle's arm, Kyle's hand on the knife, his eye on the target.

Together, they launched the relic.

"Bullseye!" Kyle shouted when the knife hit its mark.

Stunned, and with a deer-in-the-headlight gaze, Cyn stood there, rooted and silent while the wolves moved along.

All eyes watched, and then the vampire slowly brought her arms up, took hold of the knife's handle with both hands, and started to pull.

Chapter 44

THE WEREWOLF ZADE HAD ATTEMPTED to pull the *Akedah* knife out of his chest as well but failed due to the lunar eclipse blocking the moon and the werewolf's source of power. But there was no such event tonight nor any evidence to suggest that a lunar eclipse would even work to weaken a vampire.

Penny considered this as she watched, noting the fear, the dread, the terror in each set of eyes that watched right along with her. But it was Richard's look of absolute horror that fueled her reaction. With the knife inches away from being free, Penny ran toward Cyn and shoved the knife's blade back in.

"This ends tonight," she said, her teeth clenched, eyes ablaze. She braced for a struggle that didn't come.

There were words, though.

Cyn gasped, "If you let go of the knife, I'll let you live."

"I'd rather hold on to the knife and watch you die."

"If I die, I'm taking you with me."

Sue Dent

The fangs struck hard and fast. Penny felt her own heart beating slower and slower as she dropped to the ground.

Cyn turned to dust beneath her.

* * *

They were too caught up in grief, too shocked to notice at first. Rodney shook a non-responsive Josh, calling him to get up. Richard cradled an equally non-responsive Penny, clutching her limp body to his chest. And Cassie stared in horror at the lifeless body of her grandmother.

Not one of them noticed the hundreds of orb-shaped lights on the horizon moving toward them, at least, not until they danced amongst them. Some changed into human form upon arrival—men, women, children. Others remained as orbs, while a few others assumed more-ethereal forms.

"The *daoine maithe*," Ceese said to Rodney's stunned look as several floated around Josh, even through him. "They're helping him."

Rodney, Ceese, and Kyle watched the knife wound heal before their eyes and drew back when Josh took a deep breath.

"Vampires don't need to breathe," Ceese reminded.

Hearing those words, Kyle quickly removed one of his cross necklaces and pressed it against Josh's forehead. To his utter delight, it didn't singe him or

Cyn No More

leave a mark. Josh pushed up onto his elbows and grinned stupidly, looked around, followed a particular fey with his eyes as it flitted around in front of his face. "Am I high? I must be 'cuz I'm hungry too."

"You're not high," Rodney assured him, helped him up to stand. "But, let's go get you something to eat." And the trio headed inside.

* * *

Kneeling and still cradling Penny's form, Richard felt a hand gently squeeze his shoulder from behind. "She did it, son," Meri said, switching from an ethereal form to a physical one. "Penny did it. Cyn no more has a hold on the *daoine maithe*. She's gone."

"Forgive me if I don't find any joy in what you're saying. Penny's dead." His voice cracked, actual tears welled and broke free, spilling down his face.

Even as he spoke, members of the fey gathered around his dear friend's limp form.

Meri reassuringly patted Richard's shoulder. "No one else dies tonight, Richard. Especially not your Penny nor your grandmother," he said to Cassie.

Just as Meri walked away, Penny's eyes flitted open. "You're alive," Richard said, overcome with relief.

Penny stood up quickly. "Is she gone?"

Richard stood to steady her. "Yes, Penny. Thanks to you."

Her face showed surprise when he spoke, and she squinted at him. "What did you just call me?"

Cassie heard, and she took note of Richard's tears and something else. "They're gone," she said. "Both sets of bite marks this time." Cassie smiled at the memory of the kiss outside the emergency room and the other kiss in her bedroom. Her Richard was back.

Meanwhile, two more ethereal forms circled Penny, and afterward, she was inclined to look at her wrist that, for a split second, felt on fire.

"I don't believe it. The mole—my cancer, it's as if it were never there."

"Cancer?" Richard repeated.

"I was going to tell you. It came back. But I guess the fey decided to take care of it for me."

"You saved them, Penny. You freed the *daoine maithe*." He looked at her with new eyes or rather old eyes with a fresh perspective. "Do you recall that night on the beach when you wanted to look beneath my ascot."

"As if it were yesterday. I relived that moment in a vision the morning after Meri cursed you."

"I did, as well. I'm guessing at that same moment. In a dream."

Cyn No More

"Except that vampires don't dream," Penny scoffed playfully.

"Maybe it wasn't a dream, then," Richard offered.

"Maybe this isn't real," Penny countered.

"Maybe we should find out."

Both leaned in closer as they spoke, and then their lips met, allowing the kiss prevented by their respective curses on that night on the beach.

At first, it was soft and caring and then more heated and sensual, a lifetime of emotion released. Both were so caught up, neither noticed Cassie as she backed away and left.

After a long moment of it, Penny pulled away.

"What is it?" Richard asked. "Is something wrong? Did I do something wrong?"

"Hardly," she said gently. "It's just that," and she looked around, "Cassie left."

Richard cringed. "Of course, what was I thinking?"

"We," Penny corrected. "What were we thinking?" She took him by his hand. "Come on. Let's go find her and explain—if we can."

* * *

Gwen stood with Brendan, mesmerized. "There are so many."

"And I dare say I recognize a few." His smile broad, he pulled one in for a bear-sized hug. "Rolland, brother, ye haven't changed at all. Aye, ye look just as I recall."

"I chose a form you would recognize."

He greeted sisters Raewyn and Sophie next and then looked around. "But, where's Christian?"

Another familiar figure stepped forward.

"Mother." He gasped at the sight of her, of the memory of her and now at the reality of her.

"You have tears, Bren," she said, wiped at them with gentle fingers. "Still so emotional."

"I've missed ye so and worried about ye even more."

"Such a strong Scottish brogue. That's new."

"I spent a lot of time there. Met my wife there," He turned slightly toward Gwen,

Mother smiled as though pleased and nodded. "Finally, someone to keep you in line."

"Aye, that she does." He studied her face. "But what has ye so worried. I c'n tell tha ye are."

"Christian. Years ago, we lost track of him. We think Zade took him, but we're not sure."

"I shall find him for ye."

"If he—still exists."

Cyn No More

At the catch in her voice, he drew her in. "Of course, he still exists. Christian was a wee bit on the wild side, but he wouldnae curse another."

"Your grandfather will be around shortly to fill you in on what he knows," she said as she pulled away.

"Grandfather?"

"Yes, he's eager to meet his namesake."

"How will I know him?

"He wears a tall hat and," she said, cleverly smiling at Gwen, "with your beard, you look just like him."

Brendan put a hand to his face and turned to see Gwen grinning wide.

Chapter 45

"YOU ATE THE ENTIRE BOX of Frosted 'O's," Kyle said as the four walked down the hall to the parlor.

"He did say he was hungry," Ceese remarked.

Rodney gave Kyle a playful shove from behind, hard enough to send him stumbling forward. "Yeah, but it's not blood he wants, so stop complaining!"

"Master Rodney," Geoffrey called out, walking into the parlor behind them. He didn't sound quite like himself.

Kyle decided his unusual tone meant trouble and whispered as he passed Rodney with the others. "Somebody's about to get it," and he punched Rodney in the arm in retaliation for the shove. Rodney was left facing the butler on his own.

"G-man, You're okay. Cyn didn't kill you. You know, I feel really bad not getting your cross back to you. I guess I just forgot—" Geoffrey's arms went up, Rodney emitted a small shriek of panic but relaxed at Geoffrey's embrace. "Oh, you wanna hug. Of course. Let's hug."

Cyn No More

"How did you find him?" Geoffrey said, breaking his hold after a moment. "How did you find my father? I've been looking for years. You found him in a day."

"Apparently," Kyle said from where he stood, "he looked in the right 'freaking' place."

"I wasn't sure I did find him. I just sent an email off, and the next thing I know, some vampire shows up to save you. Where is he anyway?"

"Out hunting, of course, and when he returns, he can rest in the coffin built by his hands.

"Well, Richard can take Josh's coffin. That was his blood on the knife that killed Cyn—one selfless act."

"Richard won't need a coffin," Cassie said, overhearing from a nearby chair. "Richard is free from his curse as well." Her tone was so flat and matter of fact, none dared to ask her for more information.

"All I know," Kyle said to Rodney, "is that I've booked our flights back to New York as you asked."

Ceese looked suddenly lost and even a little frightened. "What?"

Rodney glared at Kyle. "I told you not to say anything yet." He turned to Ceese. "I've got to get back to my studies. And besides, you don't need me anymore. You've got Joachim, Richard, Brendan."

Ceese shook her head, not understanding as she backed away toward the front door.

"Wait, Ceese, where are you going?" Rodney asked.

"Does it matter?" She pulled the door closed behind her as she left.

Richard and Penny entered through the servants' entrance in the back of the room.

"Cassie," Penny said and walked over to where her granddaughter sat. "Can Richard and I talk to you?"

Cassie stood and crossed her arms in front of her. "I got the message," she said coolly. "You two were meant to be together."

Richard took a tentative step toward her. "I never meant to hurt you, Cassie. That was never my intention. All I can say is that you look so much like Penny, your mannerisms, everything. I just—I got caught up. I'm sorry."

"Sure," Cassie nodded with a weak smile. "I understand."

Brendan entered the front door with Gwen. "The *daoine maithe* have gone, and there's a car coming down the lane. Are any of ye expecting company?"

* * *

Clayton Henderson sat down on the forest floor just outside his cave hide-away and eagerly opened his package. He shot off a message to Lucien to let him know he had received it. He also texted him as he assembled the gun to make sure he put it together

270

correctly, even though Lucien had provided detailed instructions. The texting stopped when Henderson had the tranquilizer gun locked and loaded with werewolf stem cells.

* * *

Geoffrey answered the knock. Darrell barged in. He dropped his carry-on luggage at the door, balled up a fist, walked over and punched Rodney clean in the jaw. Rodney, seeing the punch coming, was able to avoid the full impact. Still, he stumbled back a step.

Cassie's eyes grew wide.

Blonde and athletically built, Darrell stood toe to toe with Rodney. "You want to ask me what that was for?" Darrell didn't wait for an answer. "It's for lying. You lied to me and about me so that Cassie wouldn't throw you out of her apartment. You had no right. Cassie deserves better than that."

"Is that true?" Cassie asked Rodney.

"Sure," Rodney said, still holding his jaw. "Whatever Prince Charming says, right?"

Darrell ignored Rodney for Cassie. "I told you he was playing you. You're just too soft-hearted."

Cassie smiled. "I'm sorry I didn't listen to you. I should have known better. But you didn't have to fly half-way around the world to tell me this."

"You weren't answering my text or returning my calls," he said and put a gentle hand to her face. That action brought a smile to Penny's lips and Richard's as well. "And also, I have something to show you. Before Rodney messed everything up, we were close to finding your mother."

"She's dead," Cassie said. "Grandmother told me."

"I have documents that dispute that claim," and he pulled a folded piece of paper from a pocket.

Cassie opened it and read. "This address is local to here—to a mental facility?" She turned toward Penny. "Mother's not dead. She's here. Did you know about this?"

"Oh snap," Rodney interrupted, Josh's cell vibrating in his pocket. He'd all but forgotten about giving Josh his phone back after charging it. He took it out and stared at the screen lit with activity.

"Why is Henderson texting you?" He didn't wait for permission to start scrolling through the messages. "It's some group text." And then Rodney remembered something. "This is one of Henderson's phones that he gave you when he took yours to trick Cassie into answering." He scrolled through faster. "Henderson's got a gun. It's loaded with werewolf stem cells? It's a laser sited tranq gun." He looked up, alarmed by what he read. "He's after Ceese."

Rodney rushed out before anyone could react, charged out the front door and across the lawn into the

Cyn No More

woods. He pushed through brush, tripped over things in his path, recovered, and ran on. He didn't want to call out to Ceese as he didn't want to alert Henderson of the rescue attempt. But where would she go?

A wolf howled. *Joachim. She's going to Joachim.* He heard the howl again and turned toward it. The red laser beamed directly in front of him and angled down. He followed its path, saw Ceese and dove. The bite of the dart told him he made it in time. Then everything went dark.